MY PASSION

Lawrence Furlin

Contents

Chapter 1

Zoe's Pov

I groaned as I woke up, the sun streaming through the crack in my curtains pulling me from my slumber. Sitting up I rubbed the sleep from my eyes, tucking my dark matted hair behind my ear as I scanned my small apartment. I didn't have a lot of money and I lived alone, but since I travelled a lot I didn't need a big place, especially when it would be only me living there.

Looking around I took note of my bedroom, my black sheets thin due to my hotter than normal body heat as they covered the double bed which was pressed against the wall. I didn't have any photos about, my shelves filled with either books or papers which were littered around the rooms in my place. Getting up I stretched, a yelp falling from my slightly uneven lips as felt my shoulder pop deliciously.

I know you're wondering who I am, let me explain. My name is Zoe Greenwoods and I am 17 years old and I have lived alone since I got kicked out at the age of 12. I know what you're thinking, what kind of parents would kick out and make their child homeless at the small age of 12. Mine did but I will explain why later.

As for what I look like I am actually taller than most females my age, my tall form making it able for me to tower over most who got on my wrong side which I admit isn't hard to do. I have long brunette locks, the colours in my thick curls ranging from pitch black to both light and dark browns with streaks of a bloody red which were entwined in the other coloured strands of my hair. My long hair fell to my mid back, it tumbling down in natural curls when I ran a brush though it. My body was toned perfectly, with the amount of running I did it meant that I was in good shape and excellent fitness. My chest size was also about a C-cup which I was proud of, and while I wasn't interested in having any relationships I was happy and confident in my body enough to do so when I was ready.

Back to why I got kicked out when I was younger, I know you are more than dying to find out. It's a shame it's not a happier story, but what to you expect when it's about a unwanted child in the family. You see I'm a werewolf, well I prefer shifter but whatever floats your boat. You see I am actually the daughter of an alpha, a very well-known one of our kind unfortunately.

I also have an older sister and a younger brother, ones I haven't seen in years. You see an alpha should be a male, one that will be able to take charge and lead the pack with their mate at their side. Sexist I know, but it has always been tradition. So you see when my father got my mother pregnant with my sister Stacy they couldn't help but be disappointed, but due to her being their first they adored and spoiled her rotten. In my view though and I'm sure many others she was a complete bitch, believing herself to be better than everyone else as she held her nose up over just about everyone.

Then my mother got pregnant with me, the family disappointment they used to call me when I still lived with them at the pack house. They hated me from the minute I was born, the fact I was just another female to them meaning they never actually saw me as their daughter, more of a mistake. Because of this I was treated like a slave, by the time I was able to walk I was bruised and beaten to do as I was told. It got worse as I got older, the labour I was given wearing me out enough that I had no friends and barely any positive interaction with others. My sister was the worst, she hated me with everything she had since she was there princess and I was merely an annoyance which took some of the light off her parents.

It was when my brother was born, Matt that things got worse for me but better for the family. I loved my brother and we got on brilliantly, he was the only one I considered family and to this day we still keep in touch by text and phone. I never told him where I was, or where I was going but we were happy. You see when my parents gave birth to him, the boy that would lead the pack and such they finally thought they had the perfectly family. A male to take everything over and a female daughter who could shift, so since I was the defect in the family I was literally one day kicked out when the neighbours weren't looking.

When I said that they were happy that Stacy could shift I meant just that, a female shifter was extremely rare in the supernatural world and still considered is. Getting the phasing gene has nothing to do with blood, genes and who your parents are as long as at least one of them is a werewolf. Female shifters were more destined then born, it was pure luck on the girls side if she grew up only to find that she had the gene to shift.

No-body knew though that at the young age of 5 I shifted for the first time and not like most did at 16, I was sitting in the woods like I normally did when it happened. I didn't tell them, I didn't want to since I had resented them from as far back as I could remember. Not even my brother knew, but while we were in contact which our parents didn't know about according to him, we didn't actually know that much about each other and our lives. It was a more call or text to make sure your safe and alive sort of thing.

So when I got kicked out I didn't scream and I didn't cry, I left to live out my life as a nomad. My brother stated that my parents had told everyone that I had run away, that they had tried looking for me only to come up short. Bunch of bloody liars, how dare they!

As well as being a very rare female wolf though I was also a pure white one, the only bits of colour on my thick coat were the black tips of my ears, the bottom end of my right paw and the end tip of my tail. I didn't know if I was the only white wolf, only that they were considered even less common than the normal black or brown wolves.

Getting up I quickly took a shower and ran a brush through my hair, leaving it to air dry as I walked to my draws and pulled out a pair of light blue panties and a bra to hold up my chest. Wondering what to wear for my first day of school I decided on a simple outfit, not wanting to stand out since it's not like I wanted to go anyway.

It wasn't just humans who had laws, we wolves did as well. I had heard around that from the other few rouges that I had come across that it was now compulsory to attend the nearest wolf school. I hated it! You see even though barely any females could shift they still had some werewolf DNA, having slightly better senses than a human like speed and such as well as being stronger in addition to being able to heal slightly quicker as well. Not as much as a shifter, but enough that they could produce a male or female shifter with a male mate.

Sighing I felt my brows crease, picking out a royal blue off the shoulder top and a simple pair of black skinny jeans. Adding a pair of converse I didn't both with any make-up except a little mascara to bring out my emerald eyes and a slash of lip-gloss.

Glancing at the clock my eyes widened when I saw I was late, grabbing my bag of books which I had packed last night I slipped an apple in my bag alone with my phone before locking up, running to the bus stop as I did so.

I had to wait quarter of an hour before it showed, the smell of other rouges immediately filling my senses as I paid for my ticket and got on the bus.

I scanned the faces quickly, seeing more werewolves than I expected all of them male of course. Another thing which was hardly heard of, a female shifter being a nomad. It was incredibly lucky for a male wolf to get a shifter for a mate, it would produce a stronger pup after all and with both my parents being wolves and with the alpha blood in my system it made senses I had better senses, my wolf being bigger as well as the fact I was a lot more powerful than most rouges I had come across. I had made it a mission to stay away from packs and I had succeeded, until this new law came out I thought bitterly.

Ignoring the shocked and stunned looks of the other male shifters I took a seat near the front, slipping in my headphones as I distracted myself with my music. As I closed my eyes, letting the music run through me I thought about how bad this was going to be. It wasn't a secret that packs hated rouges unless they turned out to be the mate of one of their females, other than that though they were treated as if a constant threat. I couldn't blame them, I could be completely and utterly vicious in my wolf form, the amount of savage rouges I have come across and had to take down meaning I was a predictor in every way. I could take down multiple opponents with ease, and if we didn't heal so quickly with the amount of fighting I had done I would have looked like an extra from a horror firm.

I sighed again, finding I have been doing that a lot lately as I could feel and hear the gossiping at the back. They knew I had shifter blood in me, but not that I was a werewolf. You see I had also learnt how to mask my scent, blunting it so I could appear to just be a normal female from a shifter family. It would make things easier; I didn't want the fuss or whispers that would come with everyone knowing I could shift.

Not realising I could hear all of their conversation since my hearing was as good as theirs they continued to talk about me, not that I cared since it really didn't bother me as much as it would bother someone else. I generally and honestly didn't care what they said, knowing I could take them all down swiftly even if I got a few bites and tears by doing so. I had faced worse than the five of them, a lot worse since they was nothing more dangerous than a group of vicious nomads who wanted nothing but blood.

Feeling the bus pull to a stop I opened my eyes and peered outside, seeing the other rouges coming off the buses as the pack who owned the land sneered in their direction. I kept my face blank, noting how all the rouges getting off were all male which really wasn't a surprize.

It was when I saw a young male rouge get off and immediately lock gazes with a small brunette that I couldn't help but let my expression soften as I watched them. Their faces both getting a look of pure adoration as they gazed at each other, the male who would no-longer be considered a rouge running towards the female who jumped into his arms. It was the perfect fairy-tale, the pack whooping as congratulations went around.

I knew though that deep down if I ever found my soul-mate, I doubted it would happen so easily as theirs did. I just didn't have that type of luck on my side, though a girl could hope for her own happily ever after.

Chapter 2

Zoe's Pov

I could feel everyone eyes on me as I hopped off the bus last, my wolf humming near the surface encase there was any sign of a threat. I loved being a wolf, having your inner animal constantly humming inside of you making it near impossible to ever feel lonely or unwanted completely. Not to mention the feeling you get when you shift, the feeling of your paws as they thump against the ground with your pace as the wind whips through your wolves coat. It's exhilarating!

Shaking my head I ignored the shocked and disgusted stares as I headed to the front desk, very aware of a few of the pack members following me carefully. They were trying to be subtle, they were doing a terrible job of it.

As the soft breeze blew my thick locks I felt the wind suddenly drop as I entered the building, running a hand through my windswept hair as I stood in front of the woman who looked to be in her late 20's as she concentrated on typing away on her computer.

"Excuse me" I said after a few minutes of not getting her attention, her body jumping slightly as she let out a yelp of surprize. I rolled my eyes at her unawareness, fighting a smirk when I felt the two pack mates that were following me move closer but staying out of sight.

"Oh, you scared me" she gasped holding her chest, my wolf-hearing picking up the quick stuttering of her heart as she did so. I smiled, immediately sensing her relaxing. I had to stifle a scoff which wanted to rise from my chest, it was amusing how she felt relaxed in my presence yet I believed I was one of the most deadliest wolves here. I had seen and been involved in so much pain and suffering then should have been possible, it was odd that I wasn't more messed up.

"Sorry, could I have my schedule please?" I asked, seemingly shocking her that I was a rouge with the rest. I didn't sense any fear coming off her and it was clear that she thought she was extremely protected with the rest around. I doubt she realised that it would take me seconds to reach out, grab her by the neck and twist my wrist to break her throat before anyone would know what was going on. I cringed at myself, what a depressing thought!

"Name?"

"Zoe Greenwoods" I stated, my expression blank as I heard the nosey students near gasp as they heard it. I rolled my eyes, my father wasn't the most important alpha out there or even here with the Midnight pack, yet I hated it whenever someone associated me with my so-called family.

"Are you Stacy's...?" she started to ask before I snapped, cringing when I realised that my father and my so-called family were here as well. It didn't take a genius to work out that they had somehow formed an alliance with the Midnight pack who owned this territory, and I knew if it wasn't for the law they would have tried to slaughter every rouge that step foot in this school. It was horrific how quickly packs seemed to judge rouges, thinking of them all as enemies and not just children who hadn't had as good of a upbringing as they obviously had.

"No, I am not related to that whore" I spat out causing her to cringe away in fear. I quickly shut my eyes, cursing when I realised she must have seen my eyes flash yellow as my wolf rose to the surface. Luckily she would think she imagined it, I mean a female shifter who was a nomad, who would believe such a thing. It was simply seen as impossible due to the female shifters being normally destined to be mated to an alpha or a power wolf, meaning families and packs wanted to keep them around.

"Careful rouge" Ah the followers have made an appearance, lovely. I bit my tongue to hold in a comment, my wolf not liking to be spoken to with such disgust meaning she was dying to get out and teach some respect! Instead I continued to bite my tongue and ignore them completely.

"Are you sure, I mean you have the same last name..." she continued confidently, obviously thinking that with the two powerful pack-members behind me she was safe. I wouldn't hurt her though, I could smell that her scent was overcome with a males meaning she was mated. I wouldn't take that from someone, it was just plan cruel to take away somebodies soul-mate and the thought alone made me sick.

"I said no ok, now please may I have my schedule?" I repeated, my voice strained with the effort it was taking me not to lash out before attacking the two boys behind me for invading my personal space. My wolf strangely though didn't think they were a threat, she was just plain pissed that they spoke to us with such...disgust and disrespect that she wanted to teach them some manners!

"Sure, I would watch your mouth though sweetheart. Remember the law doesn't state that the pack have to allow you on their territory if you become violent" the woman stated matter-of-factly, her eyes filled with warning causing me to have to again bite my tongue. My wolf couldn't do threats, the woman was lucky to be alive I thought bitterly as I took subtle but calming breaths to prevent me from phrasing in front of everyone here. I did not need the questions and hassle that it would bring me in the long run.

Opening my eyes having closed them to control the yellow tinge I knew had been visible I took the folder before flicking through it, taking note that none of my classes had anything to do with phasing since no-one knew I was actually capable. I wanted to keep it that was for as long as possible.

Quickly making my way to my first class which happened to be wolf history believe it or not I entered the room only to find it empty, well other than the rouge at the front who didn't bother to look up as I came in. Deciding to take a seat at the back left hand corner next to the large open window I took a seat, my music still playing just softly enough for me to hear as I took out my books. Once I did so I slumped back into my chair, gazing out the window I blanked everything out while watching the small birdbath in the gardens outside, a number of small birds bathing in the water as it stood in the sun.

It wasn't long until I felt my wolf stirring, knowing others were entering the class. It was when I felt a pull in my chest I started to pay attention, me being a female meant I would feel the mating pull before my mate did. I smiled softly, finally realising that my mate was in the same room with me and I couldn't wait to meet him. That was my first thought anyway until my heart started to painfully break when I heard him talk with his mates, it clearly being about me as I sat slumped and huddled on my own in the corner.

"Uh what is that smell guys?" one of them started, obviously looking in my direction as I kept my gaze focused on the few birds which had decided to bathe today under the rays of the sun.

"Probably that rouge, filthy things"

"She looks hot though, for a nomad" ah, that was my soul-mate, my imprint, my mate as he talked about me unaware that I could hear every word that passed his lips. While they would be less than hushed whispers to any other female in the room including the teacher, with me being a female shifter and such I could hear just as clearly as a male would.

"Dude I can't believe you said that, you would seriously bang a rouge?" another one of his friends asked, his tone holding a whole new level of disgust. I suddenly found myself listening, knowing whatever he said was going to break my heart but needing to hear the husky tone of his voice again, even if it would be causing me pain.

"Don't make me sick, though can you smell that guys?" he asked, the pure revulsion in his voice at the thought of touching me making me bit my lip to keep in a sob. I never cried, but then again I had never been rejected so quickly and easily by my apparent soul-mate either.

"What? The rouge?"

"No, I don't think so" Uh...god his voice! It was a shame he was so repulsed by my mere presence, my eyes misting over as I realised along with my wolf that I was in fact going to be tossed aside by the person who was meant to love me completely and unconditionally.

"Want to upset the rouge, you know see what it takes to make her snap?" god, I was really beginning to hate this guy. Why couldn't they pick on the one sitting in front? I snorted internally, knowing why since if they provoked a shifter and they retaliated it could cause a lot of problems at the school and for the pack. I doubted they realised it was just what they were doing to me, though if they bit I was going to bite back and I would start with this idiot.

"Sure" oh he sounded incredible, my wolf purring and howling as his smell intensified as they moved over a table so they were nearer to me.

My inner melt down though was interrupted when a number of paper balls were thrown in my direction, the teacher letting it occur making me come to the conclusion that one of them was the alpha of the pack...just great! Just what I needed it thought bitterly.

I ignored them, I ignored the curses they sent my way. I didn't react when they insulted me, trying to pick a weak stop with their comments as they continued to throw things my way without a second thought to how I might be taking it. I blacked it out, much like how I dealt with most of my feelings that weren't anger.

"Why won't she do anything?" his husky voice stated, my wolf purring as I heard it. If it wasn't for the fact he was blatantly breaking both our hearts I would have probably jumped him already, his smell....his voice, just yum! But no, it didn't bother me what his pack mates threw my way, I could deal with that. But every insult, every dig at my apparent faults felt like a knife ripping through my heart each time the hurtful words fell out of his mouth.

I never knew whether I had wanted a mate or not, but the thought that someone was out there that would love you, protect you and adore you with everything they had made me melt inside and crave for it. But now I knew he was so close, of how similar he seemed to be with my disowned parents I couldn't help but feel as if I had lost my happily-ever-after since it was now the last thing I wanted.

I inhaled sharply and quickly threw my teeth as I felt a bucket of water suddenly chucked over my head, the freezing water running down my hair and face as it soaked my clothes making me relieved that I had chosen dark clothes to wear today.

The class laughed which didn't surprize me, the rouge upfront had apparently got in good with a few people so didn't seem offended with their words as they threw them at me. The teacher again ignored everything, my teeth gritting when I heard her laughing at my expense. What sort of person does that?

I could feel the little make-up I had worn running down my face as I closed my eyes to take deep breaths to control my wolf. I bit my tongue hard enough to cause it to bleed, hearing my so-called mate breath in sharply as I did so. I knew he could sense my blood, his wolf raging since he had already seen his mate in me. He ignored it though, continuing to laugh at my expense though it seemed less real and more forced as he did so. It was his next comment though that would stick with me, the one which caused the vicious wolf in me to whimper back as his voice sliced straight through my heart causing me to grip the table as I tried to get over the pain until I blocked it out, completely leaving me feeling dead inside.

"Aw, is the little rouge wet? Why don't you just go bitch, no-one is ever going to want you, I mean who would? Look at you! I pity the fool who gets a skank with a face and body like yours as a mate, imagine waking up to that every day of your life?" he laughed with the class, though I could tell it was missing any emotion, like he had forced himself to do so. That didn't resister to me though, I had to get out of there!

I sighed getting up, quickly putting my damp books in my bag as my chair scrapped back with the force of my move. I let my damp and now matted hair hang down my cheeks as I headed towards the door, aware that the room had gone silent as I did so.

I put my hands in my pockets, walking towards the exit of the room as I did so. I paused though, letting my watery eyes meet the deep hazel coloured ones of my mates as I felt him tense as he started at me, his wolf rising with the urge not to mark and claim his mate as his eyes tinted yellow.

"Where's the fun in that?" I asked bitterly, letting all the heartbreak and pain he had caused me leak into my words. I could tell it hit home, his face crumbling in a painful expression as he flinched away from my gaze, his pack-mate still looking at him curiously as I walked out the room. As if I wanted a mate anyway...

You would have jumped him the second you realised if he hadn't basically just ripped your heart out my wolf commented causing my to laugh bitterly.

Don't forget he rejected you to darling I stated with a sob, effectively shutting her up as I did so.

And that people was how I ended up leaving my first day of school, both pissed and completely and utterly heartbroken. It was decided, I would stay away and lick my wounds for a few days before returning, damn him if he can scare me away so easily!

Chapter 3

Hunter's Pov

I woke up grinning, my face buried in my large and plush pillows which decorated my bed as I heard the rest of the pack moving around as they got ready for yet another day of school.

Let me introduce myself, my name is Hunter Silver and I am 18 years old and the alpha of the Midnight pack. Since my father stepped down and moved from the pack house down the road with my mother, his mate, I was given my birth-right of running the pack. I was good at it, strict but fair and since I have been in charge things have run smoothly.

My life was near perfect, I got treated with the utmost respect that I deserved and was feared around the world due to both mine and previously my dad's leadership. I also practically ran the school, meaning that everyone in my territory had to obey any demands I may order quickly unless they wanted to be on the receiving end of my sour mood. I had been told when I looked furious it was enough for their inner wolves to shun back at the sight, let alone the power I seem to radiate.

As for what I look like I knew I was more than good-looking, my ability to get any girl I desired at the flick of my wrist only adding to my rather large ego. My slightly tanned skin made my pitch black hair stand out, the short cut framing my strong and masculine features as well as bringing out my deep hazel eyes which seemed to make girls go weak-kneed. Not that I was complaining, hell no!

"Get up mate, school starts and you need to be there to calm the pack when the rouges come" my beta stated as he poked his head through my door, his mate Molly pressed against his side as he did so which wasn't a surprize. He said he didn't feel whole unless he was with her, a fact that I was extremely jealous of even if I tried not to let it show.

"Whatever Collin" I muttered under my breath as I face planted the pillow again, but of course he heard as he left to get ready with the others.

While I had stated that my life was perfect one thing was missing. My mate. I hated that I didn't have a mate by my side, a girl who was destined to be with me as she would take her place as the alpha female and never leave my side if I had anything to do with it. Being an alpha I was possessive of what was mine, god I wanted a mate!

Most of my pack had already mated, the ones who hadn't hoping that some of the rouges coming may be their destined mate and they could have a change of happiness. I snorted, I hated rouges much like my already mated pack-mates, they were a threat and if it was up to me I wouldn't have allowed them to step food on my territory! But no, this new law passed meant that all werewolves, including rouges in the area had to attend MY school for at least a year.

Getting up I quickly got dressed after taking a shower, grabbing my school bag as I made my way into the kitchen where most of my mates were.

"Morning alpha" Collin grinned, kissing his mates cheek as he did so. Collin was only a few centimetres at the most shorter than me, his blonde dusty hair matching his mates honey blonde curls as they reached the tips of her shoulders. She was shorter than most, but fit into his side perfectly and ever since they met they have been inseparable. I craved that, while I had the nickname of a womaniser I would give it all up for a mate of my own.

"Morning" I grunted, grabbing some cereal before sitting down.

"You seen Stacy this morning?" Jack asked as he tried to purse him lips as not to laugh, my hateful look enough for him to bite his tongue.

"Don't even start" I hissed as I scooped a helpful spoon of cereal into my mouth as my pack mates both laughed and sent me sympathetic glances at my comment.

Let me explain. Basically every alpha dreams of having a female shifter as a mate, and since Stacy happens to be the only female who could shift in our school and pack it meant that both her mother and father had been trying to push me to mate with her. I didn't want to, I hated her with a passion. While she was pretty and knew it, having slept with basically everyone due to all the wolves wanting to get it on with a female shifter so they could boast about it. It was ridiculous, not to mention she had gotten it in her head that we were actually mates and that my wolf wasn't ready for it yet which is why I hadn't admitted it. I scoffed, even the thought of being with her made my wolf hiss in displeasure and I was 100% with him.

"Sorry mate, but you have to admit it's funny" Jack continued, his tone filled with mirth.

"Leave him alone, it's not his fault the slut wants him" Chloe laughed as she slapped his chest, jealously again running through me as I watched the mated pair. I wanted that, my wolf wanted that!

"I know babe, but come on...." He trailed off, his gaze looking at hers with adoration as the expression was mirrored.

"Where's everyone else?" I asked as I quickly washed up my dish, catching my reflection as I did so. God I looked good today.

"Jack, Josh and Liam are already at school with their mates. You know that Jack is hoping to catch sight of someone, whoever that is" Collin said shaking his head, not knowing what had gotten into that boy.

Both Stacy and Jack lived here much to my dismay. While I got along well with Jack, the boy not wanting any responsibility much to his parents dismay was one of my closest friends while Stacy still had in in her mind that she was my mate. It was ridiculous, I mean my wolf couldn't stand anything about her.

"Fine come on, we need to turn up before the rouges" I stated as I made my way out to my car, grinning when I saw my other pack mates heading to theirs. I loved my car, being the son of the past-alpha had its perks since my family was loaded and I was their only child. I wouldn't have it any other way.

Pulling out of the drive I made my way to school my music blaring as I speeded and weaved through the dull traffic as I got their quickly. Being the alpha I needed to be their early encase any of the rouges turned vicious, stupid law.

"They arrived yet?" I shouted as I locked my car, walking over to Jack, Josh and Liam. It was clear they had sent their mates inside, if a fight was to break out then they wanted they away from where they could get hurt.

"Now coming in" Jack stated hopefully causing me to frown, what the hell?

I watched carefully as a the male shifters got off the buses when they stopped, the humans not knowing that this was in fact a werewolf school as they gazed at the large mansion like building with jealousy and awe. I shook my head, humans.

"Holy shit, is that a girl?" Liam hissed, everyone's head snapping in the direction he was looking. He was right, a tall brunette stepping out of the bus as she scanned her surroundings, never lingering on anything for long.

She was...gorgeous to say the least. Her hair thick and filled with shades and shades of dark colour, her body toned and her legs and chest...just uh! Holy hell what was I doing? Was I seriously checking out a rouge?

"She's not a shifter" Jack stated causing us all to scoff, of course she wasn't!

"State the obvious" Josh snorted, punching him on the shoulder as he did so.

"I know, but just look at her....wow" he stated in aware, didn't he have a mate I thought bitterly as I stifled a growl which worked its way from my throat. Where did that reaction come from, and why was my wolf growling inside of me? I shook my head, clearing my thoughts.

"Don't let Hannah catch you saying that" I chucked which immediately got the reaction I expected.

"Oh shit, look you can't tell her. Her favourite punishment is withholding sex" he stated, actually whimpering at the thought of being denied her causing me to chuckle humouressly at his expense. I got a glare in return but it only increased by mood.

"Follow her" I stated to Liam and Josh, giving them a look which stated to keep an eye on her but stay out of sight. As the rest of the rouges got out I couldn't help but think back to the girl, what the hell was she doing as a rouge? Females were respected in a pack, even the ones that didn't shift since it was an extremely high chance that they could have been mated to another shifter.

Shaking my head I made my way into school, my closest pack mates following since they would normally wait for me to make a move before they did, a show of respect on their end.

I could hear the whispers which went around the school already about the female rouge, their comments ranging from 'poor thing, how has she survived' to 'stupid bitch, getting everyone's attention'. The last one was obviously from the jealous unmated females who had taken in her rather...appealing appearance. I growled aloud at the thoughts, a few of the students around me flinching before rushing off to class causing me to smirk but roll my eyes.

Getting to class slightly late, not like the teachers cared I felt myself stop and stand rigid as the most amazing smell filtered into my senses...oh god my wolf was screaming at me to follow the delicious trail of what smelled like mangoes strangely enough.

Entering history I saw Collin, Josh and Liam sitting in our usual seats, my nostrils flaring as I tried to figure out what the hell the scent was. I could hear them all talking as I approached, not being able to stop asking the question which was at the forefront of my mind.

"Any you guys smell that?" I asked, my eyes widening when I took note of the slightly husky quality which had seemed to sneak into my tone. My question had immediately got all of their attention, their eyes sparklingly as amusement flickered through their gazes.

"Probably the rouge, filthy things" Josh stated though he made sure to keep his tone quiet enough for her not to hear. I didn't know why he bothered; he hated them more than I did since he had nearly lost his mate when we had an attack a few months ago. Ever since he had harboured a huge hate for them, which was understandable.

"She looks hot though, for a nomad" I found myself saying, my eyes trailing towards her huddled figure in the corner. It was when they asked would I seriously bang her I tried to keep the pure lust as I imagined it out of my head as I replied, successfully making it sound like I would rather be sick than touch her. It wouldn't do me well to be caught lusting after a rouge, not good at all, especially when

Stacy would catch wind of it. I may dislike rouges, but I didn't want any harm to come to the girl who obviously didn't want to be here just due to a few stupid feelings which he placed down to the fact he hadn't gotten laid in a while.

When Josh asked amusingly to try and tempt her to see how long it took her to snap I found myself replying, my thoughts elsewhere as I attempted to put together my feelings...and why was my wolf literally purring as we moved closer to her?

I didn't pay attention as they seemed to be enjoying themselves, the teacher glancing in our direction only to give me a respected nod before ignoring our antics like she always did.

"Why won't she do anything?" I found myself mumbling, ignoring how enraged my wolf seemed to be as I let my pack mates have their fun. It didn't help that I felt a pang in my heart as I watched her stare out the window, I had yet to her face but I knew she would most likely be pretty if her body was any indication.

"I have an idea" I heard Josh mumble, quickly rising from his seat as he made his way to the small sink which was placed in the corner of the class room. I felt my brows frown as I realised his train of thought, it was a bit much wasn't it?

It was when he walked back to the girl I found my back straightening, my wolf trying to rise of the service as I gripped the table to stop pouncing on one of my best mates. What the hell was wrong with me? I felt my anger, confusion and frustration rise, and as the class laughed at the now soaked girl as she made her way out of the room I couldn't help but feel it increase, fuelling my next comment.

"Aw, is the little rouge wet? Why don't you go bitch, no-one is ever going to want you, I mean who would? Look at you! I pity the fool who gets a skank with a face and body likes yours as a mate, imagine waking up to that every day of your life?" I laughed with the class, though there was no humour in it. I had to practically force the words out, and while they seemed to amuse everyone else I found myself clutching my heart as it clenched painfully.

My comment which I had immediately regretted as it fell from my lips seemed to be her breaking point, her strides stopping as she got to the door and what happened next I knew would change my life.

As she looked my way I was immediately sucked into her deep emerald eyes which shined almost too much as she looked at me with pure pain and agony. I felt my face fall, my body going slump as surveyed the damage I had done to the girl who I was meant to love and cherish.

"Where's the fun it that?" she asked, her tone sounded...dead. I felt myself flinch at not only her tone but the look in her eyes, the look I put there. I was frozen in my seat, not being able to move as she fled the room as I finally put it all together. The scent which made my body yearn to be near, how each comment him or his friends throw at her seemed to painfully clench at his heart, how he had lusted after her the second he saw her and craved to be near her presence.

He had just found his mate...and lost her all in one day.

Chapter 4

Hunters Pov

He felt as if his skin was crawling, his ears ringing constantly as his inner wolf howled and cried out for the mate he knew he had.

It had been almost a an entire week since he had finally discovered his soul-mate in the attractive looking girl who he had treated so harshly with his friends, he couldn't however much he tried get the image of her pain stricken face out of his head. It seemed to repeat over and over again in his mind as if his wolf was punishing him for not following his instincts in the first place.

What the hell was he going to do? The thought that she had left and wasn't coming back scared the hell out of him, once an alpha wolf found his mate the need to claim and be with her constantly was stronger than anything he had imagined when his dad had explained it to him.

Zoe

He had found out her name from the secretary, apparently she had the last name of the only female shifter in the school and practically bitten her head off when she even considered it to the girl. He smirked, though it soon turned into his usual scowl when he internally kicked himself at how he had acted towards her.

"You already mate?" Jack asked cautiously, the entire back had been tip-toeing around him since he spilled the beans and now his harsh mood was at an entire new level according to the mind of his beta. Most tried to keep away from him, his wolf already to the surface as all he couldn't think about was the raven haired girl.

"What do you think?" I growled out at the slightly shorter boy in front of me, taking note with a scoff at how he took a few steps back at my tone. You would have thought with him having alpha blood in him he would have stood his ground more, but he knew Jack hated it when people brought up his blood.

"Look mate did you get the name of the girl?" he asked suddenly, scratching the back of his neck as he looked anywhere but at me. I stared at him with a raised brow, why the hell did he want to know that?

"Yes" was my flat reply causing his eyes to widen slightly.

"And...." He pressed, causing my thoughts to drift to what I could remember about her. I wish I had listened to the signals sooner and took the time to take her in since I could barely remember anything else but her curves. I knew she was hot, that much was clear but I had been so concentrated on how my wolf was acting that it affected my normally very observant mood.

"Zoe" I stated, my tone growing quiet as I felt my eyes glaze over as I thought of her. I growled, rubbing my face in my hands as I sat on the corner of my bed with my head down. What was I going to do? He knew he couldn't live without her, when a wolf meets their mate they have no choice but to claim them eventually or the wolf would go mad. It normally wasn't a problem, seeing as how a wolfs mate should be their perfect match in every way, but he had to fuck that up didn't he?

"Zoe?" Jack suddenly questioned, his eyes wide as if he couldn't believe what he was hearing.

"Yes, why?" I asked with narrowed eyes, if he knew something then I was going to get it out of him whether he was willing or not.

"Shit! Crap...what's her surname?" he asked, running his hand through his hair. His sudden change of attitude had me interested, my back straightening up as I watched him with keen eyes. He knew something.

"Strangely the same as yours, but that's ridiculous isn't it..." I trailed off only to have my eyes widen when I saw the hopeful look on his face as his eyes shone with recognition. It was then I remembered that both him and Stacy did have a sister who ran away when she was younger, why I didn't know since Stacy was spoilt even more than I was.

"Wow" he breathed, my eyes widening and I was in front of him in a second, my tall height meaning I could look down on him slight to make myself look even more intimidating.

"You know where she is right?" I asked, my eyes shining with hope but my voice was rough and harsh. My wolf was inching for anything to do with my mate; I needed her more than I cared to admit.

"I can't believe you treated her like that" Jack said suddenly furious as something clicked in his head, but the next thing he knew I had my hand wrapped around his throat as I shoved him up against the wall causing him to grunt out in both surprize and pain.

"You WILL tell me where she is, remember your place Jack" I seethed, my voice filled with my Alpha command making it impossible for him to resist what I asked even if he wanted to. It worked on everyone; even if they didn't shift I was able to command them as long as they were part of my pack.

"I...I can't breathe" Jack managed to gasp out, his arms still by his sides but his hands twitched with the effort not to try and pull himself out of my grasp. He knew it was useless, that it would only enrage me further if he attempted to get away. I smirked, he was smarter than I gave him credit for.

"Talk" I spat, loosening my hold enough for him to slump but never releasing my grip. I may trust him, he is one of my closest friends after all, but that didn't mean my mate came before him. If he had information on where she was, then I wanted to know it whether he thought it was relevant or not.

"I didn't see her but I think she's my sister" Jack breathed out, the command setting in meaning he had no choice but to answer, even if he looked pained.

"You're sister?" I asked dumb folded, finally releasing him from my grip as I paced my room while he caught his breath as he panted against the wall. I rolled my eyes, if he hadn't of stalled then he wouldn't have been on the receiving end of my command. Simple really.

"Yea...she mention she was starting a new school, it was why I was eager to get going the first day" he explained, only confusing me further. I quickly spun around to face him, snorting when I saw him still sprawled out on the floor as he leant back against my deep green walls.

"I thought you said she went missing?" I asked with a frown, was he lying to me?

"Bullshit" he scoffed, "She got kicked out when she was younger, we keep in touch but only to make sure were alive if you know what I mean" he stated but the only words reassured to me where that she got kicked out! How dare they kick out my mate!

I could feel myself shaking in anger, my eyes flashing a dangerous yellow as I saw Jack quickly scramble up while backing away from me slowly and cautiously. I would have laughed if I wasn't so pissed, how dare his parents kick out my soul-mate? What the hell were they thinking, even if she hadn't of been my mate she was still a female which meant she should never have been a rouge in the first place. Didn't they know how dangerous it was out there, especially for one of our kind?

"They KICKED her out!" I snarled at him, my tone filled with pure rage as I tried to hold off the urge to track down his parents and rip my canines into their pathetic throats. Well I thought, my respect for them was gone.

"Look mate it's in the past, but you really need to calm down" Jack tried to reason but it had no effect, that was until his next comment "I can help you, me and Zoe get on well considering the situation but I can help you win her over" he quickly stated, effectively calming me down enough to stop shaking. I didn't realise how close I had been to phasing, the last thing I needed was to rip up my room if I shifted into my wolf form in here. My room was big, but I was a very impressive size for a wolf thanks to my alpha genes.

"You'll help me win her over?" I repeated, my tone still harsh but I could feel the hope bloom inside of me at his suggestion.

"Yep mate, I'll help ya" Jack stated, knowing that if he wanted to get the pack back to the relaxing mood it had previously been he had to help me win his sister over. I sighed, I could only hope she gave second chances.

Chapter 5

- -

Zoe's Pov

I could already feel the pull in my chest, the pull a wolf like myself would feel when they were away from their mate for a large period of time. The separate was never nice I had heard, and from the one rouge mated pair I had come across in my travels they had stated that unless you with them you could never feel whole. I didn't like the feeling, though I would take it over having him break my heart again gladly.

It had only been three days but it felt like a life-time had passed, the way my wolf would howl and whimper at how we had been treated, yet even so she craved to be loved and accepted by the one we were meant to be destined for.

I sighed as I rubbed my face with my hands, I was sitting in the middle of my small apartment as I felt my breaths come out in short, sharp pants as I thought about the boy who invaded my thoughts constantly. I hadn't even gotten a good look at him, only that his hazel eyes haunted my dreams and nightmares whether I was a awake or asleep.

I shook my head, never had I felt so weak and out of control and I cursed the bastard who made me feel this way. As if I wanted to be with him anyway, why would I want anything to do with a pack who got pleasure in bullying a young girl who was trying to keep to herself? It was disgusting and I couldn't believe there alpha had allowed it, then again I knew he was a jerk.

Getting up I stormed into the shower, I had had enough time to lick my wounds and it was about time I went back to face my problems head-on. I would just ignore him, I could do that I thought as I put on a determined expression before getting ready for bed. I would just blank him out, as if he didn't exist.

The following morning I reluctantly got ready for school, straightened my thick raven hair as I bit my lip nervously as I stared at my reflection. All my previous determination seemed to have run off somewhere last night when I slept, since I was feeling nothing but nervousness as thought of the day ahead of me.

I decided to dress simple today, slipping on grey pleaded skirt which hugged my hips and flared out mid-thigh. I matched it was a black tank-top and a loose cardigan, I wasn't a slut, it was just wolves tended to run on a high heat meaning wearing thick or a lot of clothes could get extremely uncomfortable. The last thing I needed to add to my list of problems was having a heatstroke in the middle of the day, even if I thought of a few who would probably love to dance on my grave. I shivered at my depressing thought, lovely.

Snorting to myself I slipped on my battered converse before grabbing my bag and music, I had a horrible day ahead of me and I wasn't exactly raring to go. Throwing some lunch into my bag, not wanting to have to suffer going to the canteen I grabbed my keys and phone before I made my way to the bus stop.

The journey was…irritating to say the least, the looks I got and the whispers was enough to already put a damper on my day. It wasn't until my phone beeped that I frowned and fumbled to find it, my brows raising when I took note of the fact it was from my brother.

Hey Z, u cumin in 2day?

I huffed as I read it, I couldn't believe I missed him yesterday. It was the only excuse to why he would be texting me, I mean he must have known that I was at his school now and I couldn't help but shake my head as I realised how quickly news seemed to spread.

Surprisingly yes, c u there bro

Was my short reply before my put my phone away, the journey was almost over and I couldn't help but feel my hands start to shake with my nerves as I tried to steady them. I hated how he had me affecting this way, I didn't even know his name for fucks sake and here I was practically shaking as I tried to settle my nerves before anyone could see me acting weak.

As soon as the bus stopped I again waited until the other rouges got off, the humans on their practically fanning themselves as they stared outside at the male wolves walking around. It wasn't a secret that we were a good looking race in general, though each of us still had our own unique look about us.

Getting off I breathed in as I scented the hair, feeling a frown forming on my lips as I picked up the scent of my so called mate. My wolf was purring in delight though I couldn't deal with this so early so I quickly, subtly dashed into the school as I made sure to miss him as I made my way to my first class, god I felt like such a coward.

The first thing I noticed when I walked into English was the stares I got, it confused me some of the reactions I seemed to elicit from them. Some were looking at me with sympathy or pity, I hated pity, while others were looking at me in awe, confusion and jealously...ok what the hell?

I grunted, I know how lady-like, as I made my way to the back corner before dumping down my things, glaring at the teacher who seemed to stare at me nervously. What was it with everyone staring at me?

"Unless you want to feel something akin to breaking bones I suggest you look the fuck away" I snapped after suffering 10 minutes of it, pleased when they flinched and quickly diverted there gazes. I couldn't help but smirk and roll my eyes, they didn't even know I could shift and I was scaring the hell out of them. I would have thought them pathetic if I didn't find it so damn amusing.

As everyone seemed to enter the room, thankfully keeping to themselves I couldn't help but feel my back straighten as I subtly took in a familiar sent. I had smelt it before, I knew that but I couldn't place it until my gaze looked with a pair of baby blues as they walked into the room.

"Jack?" I shouted, not caring that I got funny looks or that the students near my flinched at my sudden tone.

I watched as he quickly scanned me over, the other lads who stood next to him doing the scam before quickly diverting their gaze, but it was hard to miss how their eyes widened with realisation. Idiots! I could tell they were most likely the jerks from the other day, my mates so-called mates. Just lovely.

"Z?" he asked stunned, as if I wasn't sitting directing across the room from him.

"Obviously, how many other girls do you have shouting your name?" I teased causing him to blush, it had been so long since I had seen my bro again. If it hadn't of been for the extremely familiar sent I remembered I would never had known it was him, how could I when I was kicked out so young.

"Whatever Z, so how you doing?" he asked as he made his way over, it didn't go past me how the two boys followed his moves and sat on the table in front of us as they did so. I rolled my eyes, protective much.

"Fine, you know..." I answered dismissively with a wave of my hand, it didn't seem to please him but he stayed quiet. "You?" I asked curiously, it was clear he was part of a pack.

"Oh I mated" he beamed happily, I kept my face blank expect for a slightly forced smile as I felt jealously burn in me. He seemed to noticed and guilt flashed across his face but I quickly answered, he had nothing to feel guilty for.

"Really, so tell me about her. It is a her right?" I asked seriously, trying to keep the mirth from my tone. I heard one of the two boys snort in front of me, rolling my eyes I smirked at Jacks stunned expression. It was strange how well we seemed to be getting on, since we had barely met.

"I'm not gay!" he shouted out a little louder then I think he expected, the class going silent as everyone turned to stare at him.

"Never said you where" I sang as I got out my notebook and pen, a smile on my lips as he flushed at my comment.

"Whatever, anyway her names Chloe and..." he trailed off, my grin never leaving my face as he explained and talked animatedly about how they met. She seemed like a nice girl and I quickly took him up on his offer to meet her at lunch, she may be a rouge but he was still her brother and she was curious about his life.

"Zoe..." Jack stated carefully, looking at me with a look which I knew meant whatever he was going to say I wasn't going to like it. I narrowed my eyes at him, the use of my full name also adding to my suspicions that I had to brace myself for the worst.

"What?" I asked bluntly, keeping my tone flat as I kept my emotions detached. I knew, I just knew it was going to be about my jerk of a mate and when he opened his mouth my train of thought was confirmed...

"Look just give him a chance Zoe, he is a really nice guy when you get to know him" Jack pleaded, truthfully I knew he just wanted his so called alpha off his back.

"If you think he's so nice then you date him" I sneered as I looked to the front, I couldn't believe he was bringing that piece of shit up. My wolf was pleading with me to listen, to find and track down my mate and submit to him. I scoffed at my thoughts, like I would do that. He may have hurt me deeply, but other than that I was trying to keep my emotions locked away. I had been successful in doing so over the years, but even thinking about his deep hazel eyes made me want to both want melt or punch something.

I heard the two in front of me scoff, the fact they weren't even trying to hide the fact that they were eavesdropping only infuriating me further. I closed my eyes; the last thing I wanted was for anyone to catch a glimpse of my eyes flashing dangerously.

"Please Zoe, he's not been himself" Jack mumbled, trying to keep his voice down as he registered the fact he had upset me with his comment. I felt my hands clench and unclench under the table, deep breaths Zoe, you can't lose it here....

"I do not care how the twat feels" I hissed out though gritted teeth, opening my now clear eyes as I connected on the desk table before I jumped slightly when a set of fists smashed down on my desk.

Looking up I was met with a blazing pair of blue eyes, my face remaining blank as whoever it was glared in my direction. I sneered, it was nothing to do with him so why was he getting involved.

"Josh leave it" I heard Jack warn, it was meant to be low enough for me not to hear, but hey they still didn't know I was a shifter so I kept my face blank as if I hadn't even seen their lips move.

"Why should I? She may be your sister but she's a selfish bitch" he hissed angrily, I got the impression that he didn't get along with rouges well. I tilted my head to the side, I doubt he realised he had raised his voice and some of the closer students looking in his direction. I could see they were shocked, I sighed.

"Great going idiot, now it will be around the whole school" I glared, hearing the bell ring I quickly gathered my things and legged it out of class before I done something that would give me away. It was hard enough to hide my scent constantly with me being angry as well. I left scowling, seeing my jerk of a mate in my line of sight as my anger and annoyance continued to consume me....what had i done to deserve this kind of bad luck?

Chapter 6

Hunters Pov

I sat nervously in class, my fingers thumping on the table as I tried to calm my erratic behaviour unsuccessfully. Jack had texted her in the morning and told me she was here when she replied, just the thought that she was in the same school somewhere and not being able to be to her was eating me alive.

I knew where she was, how could I not when I asked for her schedule the day I acted foolish. What? I wasn't a stalker; she was my mate and I had a right to know where she was in-case anything happened. Ok that was mostly a major lie, it comforted both me and my wolf to know her whereabouts but the fact I was purposely having to stay away to give her space was slowly killing me inside.

"You alright mate?" Collin asked from my side, Ellie his mate paying attention to the teacher as he roamed on and on about something or other. I would have paid attention but I had bigger things on my mind then what I was meant to be learning in class, like a certain mate I had to gain the trust of after breaking it so quickly.

"No I'm not, my mate is in another room and hates my guts" I hissed out annoyed, my eyes flashing causing him to cringe slightly. I shot him an apologetic look but didn't say anything, being an alpha meant it was a lot easier for my anger to get the better of me and my wolf to come out. I sighed again when I recalled my dad's words: Your mate will calm that side of you, your wolf will want nothing more than to please her. I cringed at my line of thought, great I was now making myself and my wolf even more depressed!

"You don't know that" he tried to look on the bright side, not that it was looking very bright at the minute. I stared at him blankly, "ok, ok so things hadn't gone according to plan"

"Really" I scoffed sarcastically "You don't say"

"But she came back didn't she, she didn't run" he concluded, my frown smoothing out slightly when I realised he was right. She could have run, and while the bond would have forced her to come back she hadn't tried. I felt hope for once, crossing my fingers that Jack would talk some sense into her.

Hearing the bell go signalling the end of the lesson I gathered my things before I felt a wave of fury run through me causing my to stiffen, my pack mates immediately going on guard as I felt the strange emotion disappear as quick as it arrived. What the...Zoe!

"Shit" I cursed as I hurried out, aware of the fact my pack was following as I breathed in and let my wolf guide me to where she was. Was she ok, I knew it had to be from her since when my father had talked about mates he had stated he could feel my mums strong emotions as if they were his own. It was a protective mechanism, a way of keeping her safe.

Hurrying across the school grounds I suddenly caught sight of her, my wolf begging me to grovel at her feet for forgiveness. It would have been amusing in another less serious situation, my wolf was normally extremely aggressive yet here he was wanting me to literally beg like the dog I am.

As I took her in I immediately felt my mouth water and the familiar feeling of lust run through me, she looked incredible in her short yet non-slutty skirt and vest top. God how much I wanted to...

"Hunter baby" I cringed, the sound of her screeching voice making my daydream shatter leaving me in a bad mood. Great, what did she want now?

"What Stacy?" I snapped, she didn't seem to notice my tone even if she flinched a little. What the hell was wrong with her?

"Oh baby I just wanted to see if you wanted to ditch the rest of school" she asked in what I thought she meant to be a seductive tone, it wasn't. I weighed my options. One I could stay here and try and talk to my mate giving both me and my wolf some interaction with her that we both needed, or two have an extremely clingy slut screeching away at me while trying to get into my pants. Yea, not exactly a hard choice....

"Bugger off Stacy" I snapped, again she didn't seem to notice or care at my tone even if I knew her wolf did. She flinched, her wolfs reaction but stupidly stayed put. I looked at Collin with a pleading look, glaring when I saw he was trying desperately not to laugh at my situation. What a bloody fantastic beta...

"Zoe come on I'm sorry" Jacks voice filtered across the field, my pack mates and myself craning our necks as we looked behind my delectable mate to see a panicked looking Jack come running up behind her.

"Really now, that's nice" she stated sarcastically, but even with the slight edge to her tone it was still the most beauty thing I had ever heard. My wolf purred at the sound, though was edgy since I could feel how annoyed and angry she was.

I scowled, he was meant to be helping the situation not making it worse!

"Please Z, he was just being a twat" he continued to plead with her, gripping her wrist slightly causing my eyes to narrow into the movement as I felt my wolf hiss as Jack pulled her back towards him. He had better know what he was doing!

"Whatever Jack..." she started to talk but I suddenly couldn't hear her thanks to the slut next to me, it was hard to believe that they were actually related, much less sisters.

"Who is that girl?" she screeched causing me and some of the back to lean away from her, my sensitive hearing making her voice sound even worse than normal. Why was she still here?

"Zoe" I found myself breathing, cringing once I did due to the jealously I suddenly saw in her eyes as I pushed her away. I didn't need my mate thinking I was interested in her sister, and while the rumour was that I slept with her a lot it was a whole bunch of crap. I wouldn't touch that if someone paid me to.

"Little bitch, you like her don't you?" she accused, her massacre clumped eyes narrowing at me as I stayed quiet. That probably wasn't the best choice since it seemed to give the answer she had been dreading, I sighed again as I ran a hand through my hair while glaring at Collin who was trying desperately to keep his laughing bottled up along with his mate.

"Leave it" I warned, not wanting her to ruin any opportunity I had but I knew it was a lost cause. Her parents wanted her to mate with me and the slut wanted the power and position of alpha female, I knew she would stop at nothing until she got it but I was no way giving in to the slut.

"You are MINE Hunter, and that little bitch will not stop that" she hissed before storming in that direction leaving me stunned, by the time I had snapped out of it I froze when I saw her hissing at Zoe in a way which made females of our world shun back...Shit.

I knew my mate wasn't a shifter that much was clear by her scent, and while it should bother me since a non-shifter alpha mate had never been heard of it didn't. I wanted her, her apparent faults as well so as I made my way over I was again frozen when the sound of a slap registered though the field causing everyone to stop and stare.

"Damn you go girl" Ellie whooped out as Stacy's shocked form hit the ground, the anger in my mates eyes making it clear that Stacy had said something which had finally made her snap out. And while I should have intervened since a rouge had acted out, her being my mate completely abolished the rules since she was my everything, hell if she wanted to beat the shit out of Stacy and it would make her happy then I would gladly let her carry on. God I was so whipped.

I watched as she seemed to close her eyes and breathe deep breaths, seemingly calming herself down before looking in Ellie's direction. Shooting her a wink which had us all confused she spun on her heel and disappeared, leaving us all stunned yet again.

"Well...good luck with that mate" Collin stated slapping me on the back, though my only thoughts were who in the world had pissed her off and how long would it take for me to get to them?

Chapter 7

Zoe's Pov

I smirked as I watched my pathetic excuse for a sister stare at me with a stunned expression as she fell to the ground from my blow, amusement running through me as well as a sick sense of pride as I saw the red imprinted mark of my hand on her right cheek. Serves her right for talking about my mate like he was hers, I may hate the idiot right now but my wolf had acted out before I could realise what was happening, I was just thankful I managed to close my eyes and calm myself before they flashed and everyone had found out. I had never had so much trouble controlling my anger before, but this whole mate thing was new to me and completely out of my safety zone.

I ran a hand through my slightly wind-swept locks as I walked away, hating myself for thinking about how incredibly ravishing my mate looked standing on the field as his scent drifted into my senses. My inner wolf was screaming at me to run to him, to press my lips against his in a way that would show him just who he belonged to...I shook the possessive thoughts from my head, well I just made this a whole lot more complicated I thought with a wince.

The following day nothing was new to begin with, I had reluctantly forgiven Jack since it really wasn't his fault but the dick who had now spread my life story around the school was lucky I was trying to keep the fact I was a shifter out of everyone's knowledge.

I wonder if he would accept me if he thought I couldn't shift I thought curiously to myself, my train of thought hatefully going back to the man who appealed in both my dreams and thoughts. I cringed, of course he wouldn't!

Give him a chance, you know you can't deny him forever my wolf pleaded with me, her comment nothing I hadn't heard before in the last few days. I sighed as I made my way into the wolf ridden school, at least I didn't have to worry about humans I thought as I tried to look on the practically non-existent bright side.

"Did you hear she's the Zoe Greenwood"

"Why does our alpha keeping looking at her like that, are they mated?"

"I can't believe it, did you hear about what she did to..."

I pursed my lips irritated as my sensitive hearing picked up on the whispers around me, the gossipers not knowing I could hear each word perfectly as they tried not to stare at me in-case I gave them the same treatment as I gave my slut of a sister.

As I chewed on the gum in my mouth I took my time getting to my first class, the fact I was the missing Greenwood as everyone was calling me was around the whole school now much like I expected it to be. Damn you twit I internally snarled as I thought about the boy whose fault this was, well I know who was just added themselves my mental list of pain I thought with a scowl.

The beginning of the morning was lame to say the least, though the scared looks I got when they mentioned the insistent with Stacy made me smirk slightly. Due to her being what they still considered the only female shifter in the school none of the girls had acted out like I had, to scared for the consequences it would bring to them or their mates.

As I tapped my nails on the table I found myself looking out the window, only to be greeted with the males as they took their lessons which shifting was necessary in. I sighed as I looked out, there was nothing wrong with me watching a bunch of muscly blokes walk around shirtless was there?

So that's what I did, I sat there and watched them as I ignored what the teacher was saying. At least being mated to the alpha meant that they left me alone, not that I was thinking about him or anything...

"Hey...can I sit here?" a girl asked nervously bringing me out of my daydream as I looked next to me to find the blonde girl from yesterday standing there nervously. I tilted my head to the side, clicking my tongue before using my foot to push the chair out from under the table.

"Knock yourself out" I winked before looking back out the window, my back stiffening as I spotted my shirtless hunk of a mate in nothing but a pair of shorts as he stood next to the teacher. "Well hello gorgeous" I purred as I stared out the window, what? he may be a jerk but even I couldn't bring myself to deny the fact he was the single hottest bloke I had ever seen.

"Urm..." hearing the girl next to me become even more nervous I looked around to find her grinning so hard I thought her face was going to break. I raised a brow, please don't tell me I had let a mentalist sit next to me, that was the last thing I needed to add to my current list of problems.

"You alright?" I asked carefully, getting a squeal in return causing the teacher to stop and look our way, when she saw the girl was talking to me she immediately went back to teaching leaving me to enjoy the perks of the jerk being my mate.

"Yep, I'm Ellie by the way" she smiled, holding her hand out for me to shake.

"Please, a girl who can whoop like you can deserves a high-five at least" I smirked, remembering her reaction to my stunt yesterday causing her to grin as we smacked hands in a completely childish manner. Neither of us seemed to care though, me introducing myself next.

"I'm Zoe, you've probably gotten most of my life from the rumours" I winked, I seemed to be doing that a lot lately I thought.

"Like I care about that, but I also know your Hunters mate" she said carefully, waving off my comment before talking about this Hunter bloke with a more cautious tone. Who the hell is Hunter?

"What?" I found myself asked, my brows raised in a gesture which clearly stated I had no idea what she was going on about.

"Hunter, your mate, the alpha" she giggled at my naïve self as I sucked in a breath before snorting when I realised who she was talking about.

"Well talk about being thick" I told myself as I slapped my forehead causing her to lose it laughing, I couldn't help but smile at the short girls antics as she tried to calm herself only to look at me and start laughing all over again.

"Your funny, we are going to get along just fine" she smiled and I found myself returning it, she seemed like the shy type but I couldn't help but think that appearances didn't prove anything. "So I hear why you slapped the skank" she asked causing my face to scrunch up at the mention of my sister.

"Aren't you meant to worship her or something?" I asked with a raised brow, my nails still drumming on the desk just to piss the teacher off more. I could tell she was going to snap at any minute and I couldn't wait to see what her reaction would be, with me being considered a dangerous rouge and such thanks to the rumours around school. That one though I didn't mind, I liked people fearing me it meant they kept their distance.

"Like I would worship her, the only thing that impresses me in a sick kind of way is the fact that she isn't pregnant yet" she snorted causing me to grin, I like this girl she had spunk.

"You can't be that surprised though can you, the guys who are desperate enough to go to her are obviously smart enough to wrap up there shit" I smirked causing her to grin in my direction, that was until she seemed to gaze out the window next to me. "So which ones yours?" I asked, knowing that she would assume I could tell she was mated by the dreamy look on her face and not that fact I could smell the strong aroma of a male on her.

"The beta Collin, him" She stated proudly pointing out the window to see an equally good-looking guy standing next to my man. Wait hold up...please tell me I did not just think of him as mine!

"He's delicious, I bet he knows just how to please you doesn't he?" I winked and laughed when I saw her blush profoundly, yep we were going to get on like a house on fire.

Chapter 8

Hunters Pov

"You're going to love me" Ellie sang as she came jogging across the field after class, Collin immediately taking her into his arms causing a bolt of jealously and envy to run through them at how easy that had it. Not that I could blame them, I was the cause of this whole mess to begin with anyway. I was about to blank her out, cruel I know but can you blame me when my mate hates my guts, before I caught the scent of Zoe on her.

"Why do you smell like her?" I asked eagerly as we walked to lunch, ignoring Josh who moped behind me with Hannah who was also giving him her favourite punishment of withholding sex. When I found out that he had in fact had the nerve to snap at my mate I couldn't have prevented my wolf coming to the surface even if I tried, in the end I made sure he knew exactly who was in charge. I knew he had an issue against rouges, I get that, but pushing my mate further away from me was not at all acceptable in my books.

"I had class with her, I like her" she beamed, her expression immediately bringing a similar grin on Collins face as we headed into the hall. We were centre of attention of course, we always were since we were the highest of the pack with me being the alpha and Collin the beta. Not everyone lived in the pack house, but those who did were understandably closer.

"Like who?" Jack butted in as he sat down with Chloe, the naturally shy girl blushing as everyone looked her way.

"Your sister silly, she is the single most hilarious person I have ever met" Ellie winked, the mention of his favourite sister bringing a smile to Jacks face.

"Your sister Zoe?" Chloe asked, Jack nodding eagerly. He had filled her in on my mate and it wasn't hard to tell she was as nervous as hell to meet her, both her and Stacy did not get on at all.

"Yep, like I said Hunter you are going to love me" she beamed, my back straightening at the thought of my mate. I immediately gave her a look which meant spill, I would hate to have to alpha order her to but this was my mate we were talking about. She was my everything and the tug in my heart was getting more and more irritating and throbbing as the days went on, I knew it would only settle down once I had mated properly with her and I found myself ready to do anything to win her over.

"Well..." I growled when she drew it out, Collin glaring at me slightly but didn't comment, even though he was my best friend and beta he knew who was in charge. "Ok, ok I kind of invited her to sit with us at lunch" she beamed, my eyes lighting up as pulled the small girl into my arms to give her a friendly hug as I whispered a thank you. Pulling away I rolled my eyes when Collin shot me a disgruntled look before taking Ellie back into his arms, I shot him a sheepish grin as I suddenly found both myself and my wolf filled with excitement and hope.

"Wait...did you say she was coming, now?" Chloe asked panicked, it was far from a secret that she was dreading meeting my mate since she feared what her reaction would be to her being her brothers mate. I had yet to tell the pack about the pathetic idiots who had made my Zoe a rouge at such a young age, I knew she would have my balls if I even thought about telling anyone else when she hadn't said it was acceptable for me to do so. The last thing I needed was for her to have any more reasons not to talk to me, let alone hit me where it hurts.

"Yep, well she should be the teacher asked to talk to her after class" Ellie stated with a slight smirk, Collin looking worriedly at me while I grinned. It was clear my mate was going to bring Ellie out of her shell more, hell he had been shocked as well as turned on when his mate whopped after Zoe had put her sister a.k.a. my stalker in her place.

"What...what's she like?" Chloe mumbled, Jack gazing at her with adoration as her tucked a tuck of her mousy brown hair behind her ear.

"Funny as hell, oh yea Hunter you need to start going to shifter classes with less clothes on" Ellie winked, Collins eyes popping out comically wide as he sent a glare my way as I raised my hands in mock surrender. Her comment seemed to shock the whole table, Liam chocking on his drink while Josh still sulked as he sat next to the mate which was currently ignoring him.

"Ellie!" Hannah gasped, covering her mouth to hide her stunned but amused expression as Collin still glared in my direction. What, I hadn't forced her to say it?

"NO! I don't mean it like that, no offence Hunter" she quickly gushed out, her cheeks flushing with a slight red as she finally realised how her comment had come out. I watched as Collin relaxed, nuzzling her neck in a possessive gesture though from the way he looked at me out of the corner of his eye I could tell he still thought he was missing something.

"None taken" I responded, still shifting in my seat as I fought the urge to look at the entrance every second to see when she was coming. What was taking her so long?

"No I mean for Zoe's sake, when we were in English watching you guys she stated, and I quote "gorgeous" when she gazed you" Ellie giggled, the rest of the female mates gushing about having an alpha female while I gloated in the praise. I was thankful that she obviously found me attractive, she hadn't displayed any of it in front of me and I was beginning to get worried.

"Thank god" I heard Collin mumbled under his breath, my even keener hearing picking it up though as I rolled my eyes in his direction. Like I would want his mate when I had my own perfect one, she would make a brilliant Alpha female I thought with pride.

"Shit...You may have a problem Hunter" Kelly, Liam's mate cringed from his side as she looked towards the entrance. We all snapped out heads in her line of sight only for annoyed growls and sighs to erupt from the table as we caught sight of the blonde bitch walking across the hall. Stacy!

"Well at least she has other things on her mind, or body" Josh cringed, obviously taking note of one of the rouges who was currently eyeing her with hunger. It wasn't a secret that she slept around, a lot, but playing with rouges like she was just to try and get a rise from me was both foolish and dangerous.

"Is she really trying to make you jealous?" Ellie scowled with disgust, since she had thankfully started to become friends with my mate she had become extremely protective of her.

"Like the slut could" a voice suddenly snorted causing us all to jump, the delicious scent of my mate wafting into my senses making me want to both purr in delight as well as to pin her down and mate with her until I had her screaming my name in pleasure.

"Zoe" I breathed, quickly looking around her see her standing there in all her beauty. God she was amazing...

"Hunter" she greeted flatly, my wolf shunning back as I felt my face fall slightly before blanking it into an expressionless mask. Ouch.

"Zoe!" Ellie squealed excitedly, clapping her hands in a childish manner as she greeted my mate. A smiled appeared on Zoe's lips, and while my wolf praised in her being happy I couldn't help but wish it was me who put it there. Soon my wolf purred, soon...

Chapter 9

Zoe's Pov

"Hunter" I replied flatly, trying to keep the all emotion from my tone. I managed it, but I couldn't help but feel like shit when I saw his face fall before he managed to blank it. UH, why was I feeling this way? I should hate him, despise him even, yet however much I tried I couldn't help but feel myself falling for him.

"Zoe!" I was snapped out of my thoughts when Ellie called my name, a smile forming on my lips as I scanned over the table to find my new grinning friend. The whole friend thing was new to me, but I knew whether I liked it or not I couldn't exactly pick up and leave like I had planned since the mating pull would be too strong, especially since we both had potent alpha blood running through our veins.

"Hey girl" I grinned, looking for a seat only to find the only empty one happened to be next to Hunter. I sighed, nipping at my lip before shrugging and taking a seat next to the fine specimen also known as my mate.

"What took you so long?" Ellie asked as she leaned on her mates shoulder, my eyes trailing over the blonde haired boy in a judging manner as I didn't bother to hide the fact I was blatantly looking him over. From the growl which rumbled in the very pissed off Hunter's chest I bit my lip as I glanced at his expression, him being pissed off was an understatement.

As I tried to subtly glance at him I couldn't help but take him in again, feeling my breathing catch quietly in my throat as I took in his strong features. It was his eyes though which got to me, the liquid hazel which seemed to look right into my soul as I shivered and looked pointedly away.

"Huh? Oh why was I so long, basically the teacher told me to sort out my attitude putting it bluntly. She looked terrified though" I rolled my eyes, waving my hand dismissively as I suddenly realised I hadn't gotten any food. I was starving!

"She what!" Hunter growled, my brow frowning when I felt a delicious shiver ran through me and my wolf purring in delight at the sound. This boy had me all kinds of messed up.

"Yep so calm yourself down big boy- I'm getting food" I stated as I patted him on the cheek before I even thought about my actions, the bolts of pleasure where our skin touched causing my eyes to darken and the urge to claim him all the more urging. Shit.

Quickly getting up I shook my head furiously, my raven locks thrashing around my face as I screwed up my face in distaste at my animal instincts before making my way over to the food line. It didn't skip my notice his reaction to my touch either, the pure hungry and lustful look he had sent my way was enough to make my legs tremble in desire.

I knew this was harder on him, with him being the present alpha and having already of accepted his position his wolf's main priority now would be to claim his mate. I respected him for not trying to mate with me forcefully, having heard of such occasions in my travels, but I knew if he did I would never forgive him, no matter what my wolf felt.

Sighing I shook my head yet again, I was finding it harder and harder not to just follow my instincts yet his words from that morning still haunted me....

Swallowing hard I tried to clear those thoughts from my mind as I made my way to the slightly busy line, hearing the apparent whispers around the room perfectly as I did so. It was when I caught the conversation including Hunter and his pack that I found my heart beating faster, my wolf purring and howling inside of me as I tried desperately to blank my expression.

"Cheer up mate" Collin stated as soon as they thought I was out of hearing range, I was too intrigued though to even bother rolling my eyes as I narrowed my eyes at the people in front of me in a threatening manner causing them to immediately shut the hell up.

"What am I going to do mate, she hates me" Oh baby, I thought as I felt my eyes soften at the pain in his voice. What was he doing to me?

"She doesn't hate you Hunter, you just need to give her time" Ellie spoke, her voice sympathetic as I continued to glare at the other students in-case they started talking again. I didn't want to miss anything, and while this conversation was painful for both me and my wolf to hear I needed to be prepared for what they said behind my back.

"Yea, you didn't exactly get off to the best of starts" another girl said softly, I had yet to be introduced to a couple of the closer pack members so I didn't know all of their names just yet.

Hearing my mate groan in frustration at the memory I zoned them out, not wanting to hear them anymore as I grabbed a tub of tomato and cheese pasta and a fork, not in the mood for a large meal. I didn't exactly have the time to eat it either, the pathetic conversation with the teacher who knew now to keep her distance away from me taking up most of my lunch break.

Paying for it to the slightly sweating woman at the till I rolled my eyes before making my way back, only to be stopped in the middle of my tracks by a none other than my spoilt sister. Great, just what I needed today.

"Look you little bitch, you may apparently be that wimp of a sister that we kicked out when you were younger but think again if you think we want to back" she hissed, her tone only loud enough for me to hear and that was pushing it. I raised a brow, un-affected by the venom in her tone as I felt my face form into a scowl.

"What makes you think I want anything to do with you?" I hissed, smirking internally when I saw panic flash though her eyes before she tried to mask it. Too late bitch, already saw the effect on you and I am loving it!

"Who wouldn't" she asked as if even the idea of it was preposterous. I scoffed, did she love herself that much? From the look on her make-up caked face I knew she was in fact completely serious.

"Well for starters me, so stay out of my life or I will do more to you then backhand you" I threatened completely serious, stepping forward into her personal space as I made myself look even more threatening. She was about an inch taller than me, but the fact that it was only due to the death-trap heels she had on her feet ruined the whole threatening effect she was going for.

I tried to control my raging wolf as I breathed in her familiar scent, my wolf despising her as well as my parents for the way they had treated me when I was little. I had never been more glad that I never told them about me being able to shift, if I had anything to do with it then they would never find out.

"Oh what you going to do huh? I am a shifter, I am respected here and what are you? A disgusting and vicious rouge" she sneered, obviously thinking she was better than everyone else due to her ability to shift. I scoffed, my eyes burning in her direction as she tried to stifle the urge to cringe back, I could see how much I unsettled her in the way she held herself. I smirked.

"Never forget that, I am a rouge which means killing you would mean nothing to me" I hissed at her, her body flinching back as she caught the venom in both my posture and my tone. She knew I was completely serious, hesitation and fear flashing through her eyes as she realised just how little I would care if she disappeared.

"Just stay away from Hunter, he's mine!" she snarled pathetically, the comment finally pushing me over the edge as I felt my fingers clench into a fist before connecting with her nose. The sound of the crunch which echoed the now silent room seemed to capture everyone's attention, the screaming and now bloody girl making a scene as she sprawled out pathetically on the floor. Did she have no shame?

"Pathetic" I spat, clenching shut my eyes as I tried not to let my eyes flash like I knew they would. I was used to having my wolf so far to the surface, so having to control myself as not to give me away was proving to be more difficult than I had first planned...

Chapter 10

Hunter's Pov

The crack ran though the hall, our eyes widening as the scent of blood filtered into our senses as we watched my mate yet again clearly breaking Stacy's nose. I didn't know why exactly, but the pure show of dominance and aggression Zoe had shown had my wolf purring and hissing in delight, obviously pleased that our mate could clearly look after herself.

She's perfect my wolf purred and I could only agree with him as I gazed at her with possession, pride and adoration. She was perfect.

It was when she started to shake slightly, it being barely visible but I could practically feel the rage which was coming off her. I frowned, knowing how her eyes were clenched shut as she tried to calm herself.

Looking around I noticed everyone was to focused to the screeching girl to take her in and I found myself worrying, I knew she wasn't a shifter due to her scent so her actions were worrying me. Was something wrong that I didn't know about?

Quickly getting up I made my way over to her, she may hate me right now but that didn't stop me from caring about her like I should. So with that thought on my mind my long strides quickly filled the gap between us, my arms quickly encircling her smaller form as I pulled her against me, immediately feeling her shaking stop.

"It's alright" I murmured into her hair as I breathed in her scent, savouring the feel of having her completely in my arms where she belonged. It was only a matter of time until she realised it herself, and I would be waiting patiently until I had earned her trust enough to give this whole mates thing a shot.

I knew she had a difficult past; she was a rouge until she met me after all. I doubt she realised that being my mate she was automatically now involved with the pack, becoming their alpha female once I have fully marked and claimed her like I craved with my whole being. She was my everything, and for the life of me I couldn't help but wonder what the hell I had been thinking when I thought my life was complete and perfect before she even came into it. The thought now just seemed completely ludicrous.

"Hunter why aren't you helping me?" Stacy screeched from the floor causing the mood to shatter as Zoe seemed to suddenly realise where she was. She had completely relaxed in my arms, and I found myself growling at the slutty blonde on the floor for interrupting the moment and making my mate feel uncomfortable enough to completely stiffen in my arms. What the hell was wrong with the bloody slut that she just had to make herself known, it was only a bloody nose for fucks sake!

"What Stacy, what do you want?" I spat at her once Zoe had made it known that she wanted to get out of my arms, however much I protested against the action I let her go knowing not to push it. The rush of warmth that had run through me, the sense of wholeness I felt and my wolf being completely calm, if not a little lustful when she was in my arms was the best feeling I had felt in my life. And then this bitch just had to ruin it due to some stupid idea that we were destined for each other, I would die before I thought the same.

"I need your help Hunter" she pouted, her eyes watering but I knew it was all an act. Knowing that I needed to help her up, being the alpha and such I reluctantly did so with a disgusted expression clearly on my face.

It was then I heard the most adorable sound in the world, a giggle coming from my right as my head snapped in Zoe's direction to find her watching my expression with amusement. I couldn't help but grin, the fact I had accidently let go of Stacy mid-way pulling her up meaning that she fell to the floor yet again with a cry.

"Brilliant" I heard my angel mutter, her hand over her mouth as she tried to smother her laughter as she looked away as not to show me he amusement in her eyes. I couldn't help but grin widely, I had made her laugh! The thought made my wolf purr in happiness, the familiar feeling of warmth running through my body making me feel as if I was literally on top of the world. I knew the feeling was going to become incredibly addictive, my mates happiness being my own.

"HUNTER" oh for fucks...I had forgotten about the suddenly hysterical girl on the floor, my features turning to distaste as I took note of how her clothes had pulled up due to her position making it extremely aware to everyone that she was in fact going commando.

Being now mated I couldn't find any other girls attractive but my mate, I could find them sexy or beautiful but I couldn't get aroused with anyone other than my Zoe. I could try, probably being able to succeed in it if I wanted it bad enough but why would I? My mate was all I needed and wanted, it was just a matter of time before she realised the same thing.

"Shut your legs Stacy and get up, it's only a broken nose" I stated with a cringe, hearing gagging behind me only to realise that Zoe must have gotten the same eye-full I had. Lovely...

"Uh that is rank, I am definitely not eating this now" I heard her grumble as she walked over to the nearest bin and threw her food inside causing me to frown, I thought she was far too skinny and the fact that it was Stacy's doing that prevented her from eating had my anger rising.

"Hunter!"

"Of for fucks sake Stacy, get up" I hissed, fed up with her shrieking as I grabbed her by the wrist to tug her up. What the hell was wrong with this girl? She was a shifter, unfortunately it meaning she thought she was above everyone else, but because of her ability to shift like us her nose was already healing. Quicker than a female that couldn't shift obviously, but she really needed to get a grip.

"Omf" she huffed as she flung herself at me, my expression turning sour especially when I saw Zoe watching from the table I was previously sitting at. Her face was blank, but her eyes told me all I needed to know. She was both amused and furious, her instincts telling her to allow my claim and rip her pathetic sister off me while her judgement was telling her otherwise. I sighed.

"Oh Hunter" she sighed dramatically, managing to get blood on my shirt. Just brilliant!

"You're healed now Stacy, so get the hell off!" I spat, shoving her away as I made my way back to my table. Just great, that had wasted most of my lunch. But while saying this I couldn't help but smile when I remembered how she my angel felt in my arms, how complete I felt with her so close...all I knew is that I wanted that, I craved that and I knew I would be doing everything in my power to make sure I make her mine like fate had destined.

Chapter 11

Zoe's Pov

The following day I found myself actually looking forward to heading to the school, something I thought I would be thinking, let alone feeling. Sighing I felt my face form into a harsh scowl when I realised the reason why, not only was it because for once in my life did I have the chance to have friends, but I also knew that both me and my wolf were wanting to see our mate.

I didn't know how to act around him any longer, I couldn't act shy since that just wasn't me. I couldn't avoid him since I was in too deep now, not to mention blanking him was difficult since every time I either looked or smelled him I wanted nothing more than to give into my desires and jump his bones right there and then.

"Pull yourself together Zoe" I hissed to myself, throwing my hair into a high ponytail since I didn't want to be bothered with it. Hell it's not like I was trying to impress anyone, my stupid jerk of a mate can just go stuff himself.

Pursing my lips I grabbed my bag and shut the door to my small apartment, glancing at my watch only to swear when I saw getting ready had taken longer than I had expected.

"Great, now I'm going to be late. Just what I needed to make my day even crappier" I found myself hissing out of nowhere, great now I'm talking to myself! Brilliant!

It didn't take me long to walk to the bus stop, but my mood only continued to sour when I realised that the only bus that actually went my route was the one I had just missed. Great, what the hell was I going to do now?

Sighing I picked my phone from my pocket, scrolling down the few contacts I had as I found Jacks number. It couldn't hurt to ring him and ask right, I knew he must have a car due to the fact my ex-parents were loaded due to the whole having alpha blood. Sigh...

As I pressed the dial tone I leant against the bus stop shelter, glaring the idiots who either whistled or hooted at my appearance. I rolled my eyes, It drove me nuts when blokes done that, I mean how old were they? Five?

"Is everything alright Zoe, why aren't you here?" Jacks voice immediately filtered through the phone, the fact I could hear my mate in the background asking to give him the 'god damn' phone making me smile despite myself.

"Shish Jack I'm not that late, I'm fine but I missed my bus" I stated. It wouldn't bother me whether he gave me a lift or not, missing a day of school really wasn't on the top of my list of things I gave a damn about.

"What, so you want a lift?" he asked causing me to roll my eyes.

"No, why else would I be ringing?" I stated while rolling my eyes yet again, a habit I realised I was doing all too much of lately.

"Alright, where do you live?" he asked causing my eyes to widen slightly in panic, I may care for my brother but I do not want him to know where I'm staying. If he knew that my mate would know and in my current situation with him I would rather he was kept in the dark. I knew he would make my brother spill the beans if Hunter used an alpha command on him, which I knew he would have no problem doing. I sighed, this was getting more and more complicated.

"Can you pick me up..." I started, giving him directions to a large store which was at least 10 miles away. I could run through the forest to get there in time to meet him and he would be none the wiser, as long as I ran but didn't shift the fact I knew how to mask my scent meant they would still be kept in the dark as long as I wanted them to be.

"Alright sis, look for the red Aston martin dbs." Jack stated causing my eyes to widen, nice car bro.

I should have known he wouldn't have wanted such a flashy car I thought as I felt my lips twist into a scowl, it vaguely recalling to me the fact I hadn't been in the best of moods lately. But could you really blame me?

"What are you doing here?" I scowled as I stared into the hazel eyes of my beaming mate, the fact he was smiling widely at me meaning it was making it difficult for me not to swoon. He was hot when he smirked sure, but his smile just made me want to jump him and take him for the ride of his life.

"I came to pick you up" he stated in a duh tone causing me to hiss, the fact his eyes darkened in desire making me want to slap him upside the head to get him in the right track of mind. Was sex all he thought about? Pig.

"I am not getting in the car with you" I stated as I crossed my arms over my chest, my jaw clenching when I saw him staring at my chest with a renewed sense of hungry. For fucks....

"You'll be late" he stated causing me to shrug, he seemed taken aback with my next comment causing me to chuckle.

"Think I care Hunter, school means nothing to me" I said honestly, though from the way his tongue flickered over his delicious looking lips I could tell he wasn't even listening to me. Oh for the love of God! Get a grip man!

"I love it when you say my name" he stated huskily causing me to throw my arms up in the air in a sign of frustration, the fact I had to resist stamping my foot like a child making me want to breathe a sigh of relief that I managed to tamper down on the urge to do so.

"Will you get your head out of the gutter for once" I snapped at him causing him to wince from the driver's seat window, the fact we had seemed to gain attention in the street not going past either one of us.

"Look Zoe I'm sorry, but will you get in the car, please" he pleaded slightly, the fact he said please being my breaking point as I sighed and made my way over to the passenger's seat. I could tell he didn't say please very often, being the Alpha meant you shouldn't have to so saying it meant a lot to me whether he realised it or not.

"So, is there a reason why my co-called brother didn't pick me up?" I asked as I put my seat belt on, the fact this was the most lush car I had ever been in making me gap with amazement as I ran my fingers over the seats and dashboard, I had never been in something so...expensive.

"I admit I may have ordered he let me get you" he stated with a wince, obviously expecting my wrath for his comment. What he didn't get though was the fact I found myself touched that he hadn't lied to me, he could have easily mentioned another excuse but he didn't. It touched me, it really did that he was being honest.

"Oh" was my simple reply, shocking him but I was too busy looking around the car to comment on his stunned expression. This was a really nice car.

"You like?" he smirked suddenly, obviously taking note of my awe as I looked around his vehicle with unhidden interest and fascination.

"Ok I hate to admit this to you of all people, but I love your car" I gushed honestly as I grinned and shot him a wink almost naturally causing me to freeze, was I getting comfortable around him now or something?

As soon as that thought ran though my head the only thing I could think was 'Shit, I'm really in deep now'

Chapter 12

Zoe's Pov

Do you know how hard it is to sit in a car with the one person you want to hate but find it impossible to do so? I doubt it, because if you did you would know it was like hell.

I want to hate him, to loath him after the harshness of his first words to me when we first met, but I was finding it impossible to do so. Not only was my wolf pleading and begging me to forgive him and allow us to be marked, but the more time I spent with him the more I was realising just how nice of a guy he really was. Not only was he hot, he was sweet, smart and I hated to admit it but he was adorable! Just looking at him made me want to go all gooey eyed and I hated it, what right did he have to make me feel this way?

"What are you thinking so hard about?" Hunter asked curiously, bringing me out of my thoughts as I removed my gaze from the car window to gaze in his direction.

"Nothing" I breathed, not wanting to admit the real issue which was on my mind. I didn't need him gloating about the effect he had on me, I had enough on my mind as it is without adding to my current list of problems.

"You know I am really sorry about what I said to you Zoe, so sorry" he admitted, sounding pained as he did so. I didn't like it, I didn't like how much he was effecting me!

I couldn't help but purse my lips, and against my better judgement I found myself looking in his direction only to frown at the painful expression on his features as he recalled that day. It didn't suit him, seeing such a strong person break down.

"I know" I mumbled. However much I wanted to I couldn't help but forgive him. It wasn't just what he said to me though, and while it hurt even to remember it, I knew he regretted his actions. I mean I had heard that he wasn't taking enjoyment in my humiliation and pain, rather seemingly distracted so the fact that I couldn't blame him continued to nag away at me.

"You know, as in you forgive me?" he asked, the pure hope in his tone making me want to cry. I nodded numbly, staring back out the window before I frowned, taking note that this wasn't the direction to the school.

"Where are you taking me?" I demanded as I glared in his direction, the sigh from his lips meaning he obviously expected things to turn this way. No shit Sherlock, what do you expect when you kidnap a girl, a bunch of bloody roses!

"Look I'm sorry but I was wondering if you wanted to spend the day together?" he asked, his voice getting gradually quieter and quieter until he was literally mumbling. Aw he looks so sweet! FUCK! Why did I keep thinking that about him? Bad Zoe, bad!

"You what?" I asked dumbstruck, what the hell was he playing at?

"Well, urm...I thought...that" he stuttered, obviously losing his nerve as his fingers clenched and unclenched on the steering wheel as he made a sharp right turn. See, now why did I have to think that was cute? What the hell was wrong with me?

"That..." I trailed off with a wave of my hand, struggling to keep the smile off my face as he continued to stutter while blushing a light shade of red. Aw!

"Look...shit ok do you want to go get something to eat with me?" he asked nervously, not looking me in the eye as he did so.

I didn't answer straight away; rather letting my choices run through my mind. It couldn't hurt could it, to just go and have something to eat, since it definitely was NOT a date. Just a rouge having lunch with the alpha of the pack, yea, that doesn't sound strange at all...

"Just this once" I stated, biting my lip hard enough to leave a sting when a bright grin formed on his lips, lighting up his already handsome features in a way that made me want nothing more than to grin with him. The familiar feeling of warmth ran through me, causing me to shiver in delight as my wolf purred at how we were pleasing our mate. I wanted to scowl but just couldn't bring myself to do so, the fact my mate didn't stop grinning when he pulled up at a fancy restaurant not helping with the fact I was trying to concentrate on my so-called hate for him.

"Here we are" he beamed, making a move to open his door before I gently gripped his wrist causing him to freeze. I tried to ignore the sparks as his head snapped in my direction, his eyes sparkling with a number of different emotions.

"Can we, can we go somewhere less..." I stated, trying to find a word to describe the restaurant he picked. I frowned when I watched his expression fall, nervousness taking the place of his excitement. Did he think I was joking, I may be a rouge but I would never get someone's hope up like that only to shatter it for a laugh. It wouldn't be funny.

"Less...?" he asked confused, aw he looked so adorable when he was worried. Just, don't ask me how a 18 year old alpha werewolf could look adorable, just don't.

"I'm not good with high standard places; can we go someone more low-key?" I asked, knowing there was no way in hell that I was going into a place like that. I wasn't like most girls, I didn't like people spending money on me and I certainly didn't do posh restaurants or expensive meals. It just wasn't me.

I watched relived as a killer smile replaced his worried expression, his nervousness gone as he breathed a breath of relief. I couldn't help but take note of how handsome it made him look, I had to bit my bottom lip as not to comment that he should smile more often.

"Sure, how does ice-cream sound?" he asked nervously, my already small smile widening even more.

"Ice-cream sounds perfect" I grinned, showing my pearly white teeth as I smiled wide. Hunter mirrored my suddenly excited mood, quickly putting his belt back on before pulling out of the car-park and heading to another destination.

The short ride was quiet but in no was uncomfortable, the radio playing low until Hunter pulled up at a small but nice looking diner. It looked sweet; it was the sort of place I would come to on my own.

"This alright?" Hunter asked hopefully as he opened my door for me, the smile never leaving his lips as he did so. I had to shake my head amused, the fact I felt on top of the world in his company making my head spin.

"It's fine" I stated as I hopped out, grabbing my bag before he shut the door.

As we made our way into the small diner his large hand found its way to the small of my back, the movement cautious on his move. When he realised I wasn't going to pull away, finding the feeling enjoyable, he grew more confident in his actions and applied more pressure as he held me in what some would say was a possessive manner.

My head was spinning, and while I remained cool and collected on the outside, inside I was a mess. Why was I doing this, letting him get so close to me? I mean I had always dreamed I would find my mate, and how Hunter was acting right now was what I had always craved in my soul-mate. If it wasn't for the bad start I think I would have already jumped him, but what I couldn't get past was how he said it in the first place. It was true wasn't it? I was a rouge; I wasn't exactly worth his time so why was he giving it to me? He couldn't possible care, could he?

Chapter 13

Hunter's Pov

I couldn't remove the grin from my face even though I attempted to do so, here I was sitting in one of my favourite diners with my soul-mate in front of me. I was relieved when she didn't seem to over react to me taking her away from the school, but being the alpha it was extremely easy to do since I ran all this territory.

Looking at her now though I couldn't help but already find myself falling for her, how could I not when she was completely perfect in my eyes? While she couldn't shift I found it didn't bother me, why would it when she was my perfect match and my equal in every way. She was mine as I was hers, she just needed to give in and accept that fact.

"You have some ice-cream right there" I smirked, my comment causing her to look up from her half full bowl with a raised brow.

"What?" she asked in a duh tone, obviously thinking I was an idiot for pointing out that fact. I shook my head chuckling, raising my hand a I pointed to the side of my mouth.

"You have some ice-cream on your lip" I chuckled, trying to keep in my laughter as I saw her narrow her eyes in my direction. It wasn't until she slowly, seductively ran that pink tongue of hers over her bottom lip, effectively getting the small mess that I felt my laughter die down as I stared at her hungrily. Hell she could make simple things like eating desert make both me and my wolf howl in desire, I wanted her! Oh did I want her!

"Did I get it?" she smirked causing me to huff, she knew exactly what she was doing to me but when her delightful laughter filled the room I couldn't help but shake my head with a smile, her mood being contagious to both me and my wolf.

"So you want to tell me why you thought it was smart to kidnap me?" she asked with a raised brow causing me to cringe at her term.

"I did not 'kidnap' you as you so delightfully put it, merely wanted to be in your company" I stated, trying to seem impassive but failing miserably. I watched as she leaned back in the booth, tilting her head to the side as she seemed to think it over.

"You confuse me" she finally spoke after what seemed like hours, when I knew it was no more than 5 minutes. I raised a brow but gestured her to go on, finding myself incredibly curious with what she had to say. Hell I would listen to whatever she had to say if it meant hearing her voice, being close to her. God I was so whipped.

"You insult me as you mate-" she stated before I made a move to interrupt her "I know, I know you didn't mean to blah, blah, blah. Anyway you seem to get over your hate for rouges yet what? You still want to be my mate even though I can't shift?" she asked, seemingly pained when she said the last part. I quickly sat up straighter, did she believe any different?

"I don't give a shit if you can phase or not Zoe, as for how I treated you at the beginning...I...I hate myself for it truly. But I want, no need you to give me a second chance Zoe, please" I practically begged, not caring if anyone heard me do so. Hell I would get on my hands and knees in front of her if it would get me back in her good books.

I didn't know what I expected when I confessed it to her my thoughts on the whole shifting aspect, but what I didn't expect was her to react so drastically to my confession. Within seconds after I had finished my comment I watched open mouthed and pained as her eyes glossed over before a sob rose from her throat, the expression in her eyes which was something akin to...adoration. I could only hope.

"Zoe? Zoe!" I shouted after her when she suddenly fled to the bathroom, having no idea what the hell I was meant to do when I could feel that she was hurting. Was it something I said to her? I quickly backtracked our conversation, not knowing what I had said to make her react in such a way.

I continued to wait for my mate as she stayed in the bathroom for what seemed like hours, though after roughly 20 minutes she came out. I felt my heart break as I took in her puffy eyes, her slightly paler face as she made her way over to me in a confident way, though the effect she was going for was ruined when I caught sight of her bloodshot emerald eyes.

"Zoe, are you ok? Did I say something? Do you want-" I started as I stood up to greet her, my eyes filled with worry as concern dropped from every word which fell from my lips.

It was then I took note of the apprehension in her eyes along with a determined expression, I was about to ask what was going on inside of that pretty head of hers when she stopped in front of me, her scent invading my senses causing my body to pulse and twitch in need.

"Once chance" was all she breathed before her small hand wrapped itself around her neck and pulled me down. I felt her heartbeat increase radically as I closed my eyes, my head tilting as I breathed in her delicious scent. All I could think was if I died right now, I would die a happy man.

Chapter 14

- -

Hunter's Pov

I couldn't wipe the grin off my face even if I tried, not that I would want to as I stood outside the school with my pack as I waited for the buses to pull in.

It had been 4 days since that night I took my angel to the ice-cream diner, the night I thought I had made things worse when I had thankfully made the right decision. I remember feeling so nervous when her brother told me about her issue with needing a ride, how I had immediately told him I was picking her up even if Jack thought it would only make things worse. I was thankful I didn't listen to him, I had shown her my softer side and I couldn't have been more relieved that I did.

"You know it is official, I have never seen you so happy" Liam stated with a smirk as his own mate stood by his side, Kelly on her phone as she played what looked like some penguin game which I couldn't help but shake my head at. Liam thought it was adorable that she was so obsessed with it, the rest of us just finding it as amusing as hell that a girl her age could be so interested by it.

"How could I not be, the rouges haven't been causing a problem, Zoe is finally giving me a shot and my wolf is practically purring with contentment" I grinned, my pack mates finding it hilarious but I didn't care. Why would I, I was finally getting a shot with my mate and while we were taking it at an extremely slow pace I was to thankful that she was even giving me a shot to be bothered by it.

"Whatever dude, I still don't like her" Josh muttered caught me to glare heavily in his direction, Hannah had nothing against my mates history so why should he? Sure it was sad that Hannah was nearly taken out, but if she can give my mate a shot then he fucking can!

"You know what will happen if you make her uncomfortable Josh, do not forget that" I hissed causing him to shudder as he recalled what happened the last time he upset her, he may be one of my closest friends but I was still his alpha and Zoe was still my mate. He needed to learn his place! He could do it the easy way, or the hard way it was up to him.

"Sorry alpha" he muttered causing me to nod and Hannah to kiss his cheek in thanks, it was amusing to watch as his face light up as he pulled her closer, and while I would have probably laughed at his display a few weeks ago I knew exactly what he was feeling thanks for my own angel, my Zoe.

"Buses are here" Jack grinned as they started to pull up, my back straitening as I pushed myself off the wall. I had tried to get her to let me give her a ride but she had refused, saying the bus journey was her thinking time which I could completely understand. I didn't want to push her after all, I knew I was a lucky fuck to get the chance she was giving me and I wasn't foolish enough to throw it away for something so trivial.

We all stood as the rouges got off the buses, ok I admit that is slightly untrue due to a large number of the rouges actually being the mates of some of our females. Because of this, like the situation I had with Zoe they were immediately connected to the pack and no longer considered a rouge, though at the next full moon there had to be a ritual for them to be mind-linked with the pack when we were in our wolf forms making it official.

"Zoe" I found myself breathing much to the amusement of my pack when I felt the ache in my chest loosen when her scent drifted into my senses, my wolf no longer pacing in my inner cage as it was calmed by our mate.

As I continued to look in her direction I found myself grinning when her form bounced down the steps of the bus, her head snapping in my direction causing my heart to flutter at the similar goofy smile she wore which was so much alike to mine.

"Morning everyone" she greeted with a killer smile as she walked into my embrace, my arms wrapping around her small waist as I pulled her against me and breathed in her all to addicting scent. Mm...

"Morning gorgeous" I breathed as I nuzzled my face in her thick curls, hearing my pack greet her as well as she relaxed in my embrace and wrapped her arms loosely around my waist, effectively pulling me closer. Hell not that I had anything against it, she could pull me as close as she wanted if it felt his good.

"So Zoe did you hear what your sister done the other day?" Ellie giggled causing my mate to sigh, the fact she was the missing Greenwoods was all around the school now and people were continuously talking about it or giving her stares. I tried my best to silence them all, but gossip was gossip. I was just glad her hearing couldn't pick up some of the whispers going around, even if sometimes I was paranoid that she could in fact pick up on what they were saying.

I couldn't help the feeling that she was hiding something from me, something big that I was completely missing. It's not like I didn't know she didn't have a great life, being kicked out at such a young age, but hoped that someday she would trust me enough to tell me about her past. It was sickening how her parents had tossed my angel aside, and I knew if they weren't on a business trip I would have immediately gone and ripped out their throats as soon as I had found out. That business trip had saved them, but they were going to feel my wrath when they got back and that was a promise I intended to keep.

"I wish you wouldn't call her that, I prefer the term slut, or whore, or whatever else you could think of" Zoe mumbled against my chest causing me to chuckle along with the rest of the pack, it was not a secret that no one liked Stacy and the only reason she was even living at MY pack house was due to my respect for her parents since they had alpha blood.

That thought made me freeze and my eyes to narrow slightly, the little respect I had for her parents was successful gone when I heard about how badly they had treated my mate, and as soon as I had the all clear from my angel to make my pack aware of how disgusted I was with them I could successfully kick them out of my territory, or kill them it depends on how badly they had treated her. Well that was my plan anyway, I had yet to introduce my mate to my parents though that was the next step on my to-do list.

Shaking the depressing but serious thoughts from my head I concentrated on the warm and complete feeling I got from my mate, who had still yet to move from my arms not that I was complaining. It was when I clued back into the conversation I realised I must have zoned out since the females were gigging and even Josh wasn't able to hide the smile which seemed to appear on his lips.

"What did I miss?" I asked curiously, Kelly snorting as she stood by Liam's side as I did so.

"Nothing much, just a very delightful overview on what Zoe thinks about her sis-sorry about the whore" Kelly corrected herself with a giggle, Liam looking at her adoringly as she did so.

"Thanks for the correction Kelly, much appreciated" Zoe mumbled causing another round on laughter to sound around the pack before we started to head inside.

"You ok?" I asked her when she made no move to let me go, again not that I was complaining or anything.

"Yea I'm fine" was all she sighed out before jumping up suddenly, surprizing me enough to only just catch her in time as she wrapped her deliciously long legs around my waist in a way which made me want to do nothing more than to mount her right there and then. She really wasn't making this whole taking it slow easy was she?

"You sure?" I asked concerned as I walked into the school where my pack mates had already gone, my hands firmly on my mates firm and perfect arse as I held her weight so she didn't have to strain her legs as she kept them wrapped around me. I wasn't complaining about the position though, hell no I LOVED the position, I just wished I wasn't having to hold myself back from stripping her down and marking her like both me and my wolf so desperately wanted to.

"I'm fine Hunter, thank you for asking though its sweet" she mumbled against my neck, her breath on my naturally hot skin making me shiver. I felt her smile against my tanned flesh, her comment making my grin even wider as I felt my heart flutter at her compliment. Yep, I was whipped.

"So you think I'm sweet huh?" I teased, I couldn't help myself.

"Yep, I think your adorable" she giggled, the sound making me pull her even closer against me as I took my time getting us to class. I had switched all mine to be with hers, so we had all our lessons together except for when I went to shifter classes to help train my pack to fight, to shift and such where I had to reluctantly leave her. It was times like that I wished she could shift, but shifter or not she was still my angel and it changed nothing about how I felt about her. She was my everything, even if she was only just beginning to realise that.

Chapter 15

Hunters Pov

I couldn't help the sigh which fell from my lips as I stood on the large field which held the shifters of our pack, the fact I had been forced to leave my angel to attend this lesson not settling well with me. My pack had been avoiding me as much as possible, not that I could really blame them since I wasn't exactly in a good mood. How could I be when my angel wasn't here, she should be at my side for fucks sake where she belonged!

I ran a hand through my hair as I glanced to my right, trying to fight a grin when I felt my mates eyes on me as I did so. I had taken Ellie's advice and immediately stripped off my shirt when I made my way onto the training field. What? I was a bloke after all and the fact I could feel some of my mates lust was a bonus!

When we mate fully we will be a lot more in-tune with each other, meaning not only will she be mine as I hers but I will be able to not only feel her emotions as if they were my own but I would be able to track her with ease. It was something I couldn't help but look forward to, being so close to her in such an intimate way was extremely pleasing to both me and my wolf.

"Hey mate snap out of it will you" Collin joked as he came jogging to my side, careful to keep his tone playful. My wolf didn't take a good view on being ordered around, Collin like the rest of the pack knew to be careful around me. My father was also similar, that thought reminding me that both he and my mother were getting antsy with wanting to meet my mate and the future alpha female once I had marked her.

"Whatever, how the hell do you cope with this?" I asked frustrated as I ran my hand through my hair yet again, keeping a close eye on the new pack mates who happened to be the rouges who had mated in the pack. The other male rouges had a different class, we weren't exactly going to teach them how to fight so they could turn on us were we?

"What being away from my Ellie?" he asked and I nodded. "It's never easy mate, in fact I bet its worse for you since your wolf is as possessive as hell, no offence" he continued causing me to scowl. Brilliant, that's just lovely news.

"Well that sucks" I stated before shrugging. Turning around I rounded everyone up before stating that we were working on speed, everyone following into the woods before I felt the familiar feeling come over me as I shifted into my pure black wolf.

Hey Hunter

I cringed when I heard Stacy's voice in my head, unfortunately it was the one place I couldn't avoid her completely. For the start I had tried to completely blank her out, ordering her to the opposite end of the field since she had been more than a little difficult lately with the whole me dating her sister and everything.

She believed I was delusional and made sure to remind me constantly, her whiny voice being more of an annoyance then anything. It was when she started to try and throw herself at me I started to tell her to back off, the last thing I needed was Zoe getting the wrong idea and losing any chance I had with her. That thought was completely unacceptable, after finding out what an amazing person she is, how my wolf as well as myself feel incredible in her presence even the thought of being away from her was not acceptable to me.

Fuck off Stacy, I'm not in the mood and unless you want to feel my teeth in your neck I would shut it and concentrate! And before you comment, I will make sure it's painful I hissed at her, baring my teeth in a way I knew made her wolf whimper. I was correct of course, hearing her whine before she scurried off causing me to roll my eyes. She may think she has power over everyone due to being the only female shifter but when I'm done with her parents she will be finding herself without a pack house and moving back in with her parents if I had anything to do with it.

Priceless mate Liam laughed, the sound in his wolf form gaining him odd looks as we all watched Stacy run off with her tail between her legs.

I rolled my eyes when I caught her thoughts, the fact she was foolish enough to think I was just playing hard to get saying it all. Seriously, why would I want her? Not only was she rude, disrespectful and believed herself to be the alpha female but it wasn't like she had the skills to be. She wasn't one of the fastest, she was lazy and undisciplined, the fact she was a good fighter not making up for the fact she didn't listen to orders unless I made her.

She needs to learn her place, I am getting sick of her I replied back with a grunt, hearing laughter around the pack minds as even the past rouges found it amusing. I was shocked but pleased at how easily they had accepted the idea of being in a pack, but it wasn't hard to realise why when they stated they didn't become rouges voluntarily, but rather were kicked out or forced to leave their past packs.

I just can't believe you said that to her, priceless Josh snorted causing me to roll my eyes, receiving weird looks as I did so since I doubted it looked exactly natural in my wolf form.

The rest of the morning went well but I soon found myself looking forward to lunch so I could be with my angel, hoping she hadn't found out that I had in fact had a word with the teacher who had tried to give my angel detention. Did she miss the fact that Zoe was her superior, the last thing the teacher should be doing was telling her what to do?

Striding into the lunch hall I was pleasantly surprised to find her already sitting at my table with the girls, my grin widening when I took note that she was in fact eating. In my eyes she was still far too skinny for my liking, I had nothing against a girl who had a little meat on her bones but I wasn't stupid enough to make my views known to her.

"Hey baby, you have a good morning?" I asked as I kissed her cheek before sitting down next to her, planning on getting something to eat a little later.

"Yep, though I heard you had a very interesting talk with one of my teachers" she hummed as she looked at me with a raised brow, the rest of my close pack mates walking in behind me as they immediately went to their mates to greet them.

With her comment I was sure I went white as a sheet, making me pleased as hell that the fact I was naturally tanned meant it would be slightly easier to hide my reaction. Shit, is she mad at me? Crap, crap I knew I shouldn't have interfered but I couldn't help myself, and I was sure I looked comical with my eyes wide and my mouth open as my pack mates laughed at my expense.

"Don't worry Hunter, I actually thought it was sweet" Zoe smiled, immediately making me relax as I breathed a dramatic sigh of relief causing laughs and chuckles to break out across the table.

"Well that's a relief, I'll be right back I need to get food. You need anything babe?" I asked her as I made a move to get up, I was starving. Werewolves had an extremely high metabolism meaning we needed to eat a LOT to keep up with how much we shifted and such.

"Could you get me a drink, a milkshake will do?" she asked, making a move to get her purse from her bag causing me to scoff. Oh hell no! She may want to take things slow but I had more than enough money then I knew what to do with so there was no way I was letting her pay for anything I could get for her. Not to mention it made both me and my wolf want to purr, the feeling I got from looking after my mate was one which I found deliciously addicting.

"Milkshake it is" I stated before walking away after kissing her cheek, leaving her sitting there open mouthed as she held the money in her hand.

I could hear my pack laughing at her expense, and while I normally wouldn't have liked it I had to admit it was amusing to hear her huff under her breath and mumble something along the lines of not being a kept woman.

That right there was another thing I loved about her, unlike Stacy she didn't seem to value money what-so-ever. She had lived without a lot of it for most of her life after all, and while the thought pained me I couldn't help but find the trait endearing that she definitely wouldn't be with me for my money alone, not that I thought she would be or anything.

"Hold up mate" Collin called as the rest of the males quickly headed to get food, the shifter lessons ending slightly later than the normal ones so it was basically all the males who were now lining up in the food isle.

"Hunter, Hunter!"

"Oh for the love of god..." I muttered as Collin shot me a sympathetic look, Stacy running into the hall with a panicked look on her face as she scanned the room for me. Spotting me in the food line she quickly made her way over, and if it wasn't for the fact she looked panicked I would have ignored her.

"What is it Stacy?" I asked annoyed causing her to frown.

"It's my parents, there...there" she stuttered out causing my brows to crease, what was wrong with the bloody twats?

"What about them Stacy?" I asked flatly, gaining odd looks from my pack mates. I knew why, it was obvious since I should have been on more of an alert. But would you care if your soul-mate, the girl who is your life, your everything was kicked out when she was a child by those people! They made me sick, disgusted even and if they hadn't of been away I would have ripped their throats out before I could have calmed down. I knew that, Jack knew that and it was only a matter of time before everyone did if my mate was ok with her past being made aware like that.

"Why aren't you more worried!" she screeched, obviously upset with my lack of reaction.

"Ok, ok Stacy I'm sorry. Tell me slowly what happened" I asked soothingly, having gained a crowd due to her heated entrance and high pitched shouting.

"Their house burnt down, I don't know how but apparently some-one set a fire" she gasped out causing my eyes to widen. Almost instinctively I looked towards my mate only to find an extremely innocent expression on her face.

"Fucking hell..." I found myself breathing in shocked awe, her eyes locking with mine as the emotions present told me all I needed to know. I didn't know whether to be impressed, amused or scared of what my mate was capable of.

"Fucking hell indeed" I heard Jack as he mumbled next to me, obviously putting two and two together. Ok, I had to admit to myself, my mate was a badass alpha female...even if it scared me to my bones how far she would go for revenge. Yep, I will definitely not be getting on her wrong side if I can help it.

Chapter 16

Zoe's Pov

    I held his stare as he stared at me shocked, my eyes must have been completely blank due to the completely stunned expression on his face. I couldn't help but wonder if he would assume it was me who did it, part of me hoping he wouldn't come to conclusions as to shatter the trust I had already started to build up with him.

"Holy shit"

"OMG"

"Is she serious?"

Murmurs whispered around the hall, the entire pack staring in my direction as I kept a blank face. Sure blame the rogue why don't they? Did they seriously have that much of an issue with me, to blame me for something they had no proof that it was me who done it?

"YOU" I think it was Josh shouted as me, pointing his finger at me accusingly causing me to raise a brow in his direction unimpressed.

"Who me?" I asked innocently, ok I won't deny the fact I was purposely trying to wind him up. It wasn't a secret to me that I had a sick sense of humour, and by the way his eyes narrowed I saw it was working just fine.

"I knew we shouldn't have trusted her! She is a rouge after all" he spat only to have my mate grab him by the collar of his shirt. Did I mention that my mate was fuck hot when he was angry, because he is and at that moment as I watched his eyes flash with his inner wolf he was the hottest I had seen him. Hello gorgeous...

"Call her a rouge one more time and see where you end up" Hunter snarled in his face, Hannah tensing as she stared at her mate with panic and worry.

"Don't worry Hannah" I smiled, seeing her relax just slightly but her eyes remained on her mate. I couldn't exactly blame her, hell she was in near tears at the scene in front of her.

"Get the bitch Hunter; she burned my parents' house down!" Stacy screeched causing me to roll my eyes, sighing I leaned on my hand as I continued to watch the scene pan out in front of me. Could she have been any more dramatic?

"Stacy, we don't know that" Hunter snarled, obviously not liking the fact his obsession had called me a bitch. Hope bloomed in my chest at the thought of him trusting me enough not to just jump to conclusions, even if I had been the one who burned the bloody house down so what? The fact they had immediately jumped to me said a lot about how untrusted I really was, I didn't know how to feel about that realisation.

"Of course we do, it's obvious" she continued to screech, I was actually impressed that she never seemed to give herself a headache with all that screaming.

I continued to listen to them argue it over, Jack staring at me with an amused expression. Whatever they may think I didn't actually burn the house down and my brother was completely aware that if I did want to take revenge on my so-called parents then I would serve as the reaper and just kill them. It may sound cruel, but I had the attitude of a rouge after all so it was hardly my fault for my line of thinking.

Sighing I ran a hand over my face before continuing to enjoy my lunch, my pleasant hum running through the canteen as everyone looked at me with expressions of both amusement and disbelief as I continued eating my lunch. I was hungry and I had already paid for it, unlike most in the hall I didn't have daddies credit card to afford to waste on my hearts desires...not that I would take it if it was offered to me, like I would want to owe that man anything!

"How can you be so calm?" Ellie whispered to me causing me to shrug, at least my new best friend didn't seem to think I was the cause of it, and while she was correct that I didn't start the fire I doubt she realised just what I was capable of when the mood strikes me.

"Don't you think it's amusing?" I asked, the side of my mouth twitching in an attempt not to smile. She gave me a look of disbelief and confusion.

"What?"

"The fact that while practically everyone seems to think I achieved it, none of you seem to have taken note of how she smells of fresh smoke meaning it happened literally minutes ago" I smirked as I took a sip from my drink, Stacy's eyes widening with panic as Hunter strode the few paces towards her before breathing in.

"How did you-"Ellie started to question causing my eyes to widen. Shit. I wasn't meant to be able to smell that on her...think Zoe....think...

"I was breathing in when she waked past, hard to miss it when she was so close" I stated with a shrug, keeping my voice casual causing them all to shrug before nodding. I stifled the sigh of relief that wanted to escape me, thank god they weren't that educated on female shifters.

"Stacy, what happened?" Hunters alpha command filled the room causing me to shiver, god he sounded so husky....yummy!

"I don't know" she mumbled in a strained voice, the alpha command obviously setting in. "I was going to my house when I saw the flames, I thought it was a good opportunity to get back at that bitch!" she hissed as she pointed at me causing my brows to raise, lovely.

"Get back at her for what?" my brother asked confused, I had an idea of where she was going with this but I kept quiet and observed.

"For stealing you from me!" Stacy screamed causing the guys to cringe back at the volume, hell even my ears were ringing slightly and I was sitting across the hall.

"OMG, she lost it" I heard Kelly whisper, I couldn't help but agree.

"We will deal with this later Stacy, and for the record I am not yours!" Hunter growled out causing my wolf to purr at the pure viciousness in it, hello Mr Big Bad Wolf...grurr!

"But, but..."

"That's an order!" he continued to snarl out causing her to lower her head in a submissive gesture as she showed her neck, her eyes showing how much she loathed the action but her wolf forcing her to do so. I wanted to roll my eyes, did she not know when to give in and accept that she needed to back down? Fool!

"Yes alpha" she whimpered before running from the room, gossip and whispers spreading around the canteen as the tense atmosphere was lifted, even if I happened to be the sudden talk of the school again as everyone debated on whether or not I was actually the cause or not of the fire and if not who was.

I watched as Hunter walked towards me, his eyes shifting from nervousness to worry. The worry confused me, what did he have to be worrying about?

"I'm sorry" he immediately whispered as he sat next to me, what the hell was he on?

"For what?" I couldn't help but ask, I was curious to what he thought he had to be sorry for.

"For jumping to conclusions and thinking it was you" he stated causing me to frown. "I know it's not though, the more I think of it the more I know that it wasn't" he continued to whisper, obviously not wanting the pack to hear him apologising. I didn't take offence, he was the alpha and the fact not only was he apologising but he was being honest and confiding in me I couldn't help but forgive him almost instantly. Fuck he had my inner walls crumbling so fast it was giving me a headache!

"Thank you" I whispered as I moved closer to him, pressing my lips to his cheek causing delicious sparks to erupt form the both of us causing our wolves to purr in delight.

"For what?" he asked, obviously confused to why I wasn't shouting at him like he had clearly expected when he had walked over.

"For being honest, for apologising, for having faith in me. You can choice which reason you like" I smiled causing a relieved expression to form on his face as his eyes brightened at my comment. It was clear my reaction was what he had been worried about.

"You are amazing" he laughed as he pulled me onto his lap, his head nuzzling my neck as the tension was broken.

"Sorry Zoe, really I just..." Josh started, the guilt in his eyes and the look he was receiving from Hannah clearing making him want to relieve some of the guilt he was feeling.

"It's fine Josh, you must have a good reason not to like rouges and I respect that." I waved off causing him to look at me in a new light; I rolled my eyes not wanting to know what was causing the boy to look so bloody conflicted.

"You are perfect" I heard Hunter whisper and it was right then I heard his feelings for me. His love, his hope, his adoration and I knew I had to come clean. I just hoped he took the whole sifter thing in his stride. Fingers crossed though that I actually had the guts to tell him, he would be the first to know after all but that's not what worried me....

Chapter 17

- -

Hunters Pov

My mate stared at me with a raised brow, her dark locks piled on top of her head as they were held in place with a large black claw clip. I couldn't help but keep brushing the small strands which she had kept down to frame her face, loving the feel of her silk locks on my fingers as I tucked them behind her adorable little ears.

I was currently running my hand through my hair yet again as I stared at my confused mate, trying to work up the courage to ask her to meet my parents and look around the pack house. I didn't want to push her to live with me, but she was my mate and I hated to think of the sort of place she was staying at now. It drove both me and my wolf nuts, knowing I should be caring and providing for her yet knowing she wouldn't allow it like I wished she would.

It had been a few days since the whole fire incident and everyone was on their guard, the scent of a rouge being near the house when we went to investigate. I wanted to strangle Stacy when we had identified it as a rouges' doing and not of my mates, yet she had dared blame her out right without bothering to check her facts and scent the area around her like she should have done! It was basic procedure to identify any scents straight away, if it had of rained they would have been washed away and we would have been left non-the-wiser. For a shifter, she could be extremely foolish sometimes.

I was brought out of my thoughts when my mates beautiful voice cut through the awkward silence which I had unfortunately built up with my stuttering, I was relieved to say the least.

"What did you want to ask me Hunter?" she asked with a slight frown, playing with a blade of grass since we were sitting on the field. She had found the perfect spot according to her, it being under a large willow tree which while gave you shade made sure you got the warm summer breeze.

"Look...you don't have to say yes...but...urm" I stuttered as I felt my tanned skin heat up with both embarrassment and frustration, why couldn't I just ask her? Oh, that's right, I was afraid she would say no and things would get awkward. God this sucks! I was the alpha for sucks sake!

"Hunter, just ask me" she smiled, the amused look in her eyes causing me to pout playfully. It was worth it though, her laughter filling the field, entrancing both myself and some of the unmated wolves around us who had turned at the airy sound of her laugh.

That was another thing which I had noticed, how my mate seemed to have captured all of their attention for some reason. Sure she was funny, sweet, sexy and incredibly badass but that didn't mean they had a shot with her! She was mine, and I knew my wolf would kill any who thought they had a claim on her.

"Will you meet my parents tonight?" I blurted out before I could help myself, already preparing myself for the rejection when I saw her stunned and taken aback expression.

"Urm...why?" she asked nervously as she avoided eye contact with me, a strange emotion on her face as she flushed an adorable red which made me again wonder how far it went down. She rarely blushed, but when she did it was just delicious to watch.

"What do you mean why?" I asked curiously, why wouldn't I want them to meet her?

"I just didn't expect to ever meet them Hunter, I mean why would you want your parents to meet a rouge who just happens to be your mate?" she asked, her voice I could tell was filled with insecurities even if she had tried to hide it behind annoyance. I sighed, grabbing her chin gently as I got her to look at me only for my thoughts on her insecurities to be confirmed as I looked into her amazingly emerald orbs.

"You are not a rouge baby, you are my mate and you have no idea how glad I am that fate had chosen my other-half to be you." I smiled with complete honestly, needing and wanting her to understand that even if I had the power to change it then it wouldn't even cross my mind, she was my everything and I was not going to ruin that.

"You too sweet" she pouted as she pushed me away playfully causing my back to hit the ground with a thud, a grunt falling from my lips at the action though I couldn't help but laugh at her stunned expression.

"Hell you have some strength there babe" I smirked only to find my thoughts whirling. That was until I saw her eyes widen slightly before she swung her leg over my waist, effectively straddling me.

My head was immediately swimming with a whole different train of thoughts, her hands going either side of my head as my hands automatically went to her hips as I stared at her lips hungrily. I couldn't help getting aroused by it, hell my gorgeous and incredibly sexy mate was on top of me in shorts, could I get a amen?

"You know you smell so good" she purred, my eyes flashing with my inner wolf as I felt her hot body temperature press against mine, the fact she ran on the same heat frequency meant that she felt nothing other than perfect in my arms. If I was thinking clearly I had a feeling I would have thought more on the topic of how it was possible she ran as hot as me, but I was way too distracted with her seductive tone and how her body felt against mine to even consider taking my mind off what was happening now.

"Uh" was all I got out as a strangled sound came from the back of my throat, god was that really my lame reply?

"Like a musky masculine scent, it's so fucking good" she almost moaned as I felt her lean down, her breath on my neck causing me to shiver and my grip on her to tighten significantly. Holy fuck, she was going to kill me!

"Really now?" I purred, my voice so low that even I couldn't recognise my own voice. I could feel her shiver against me as I spoke, I smirked, loving the effect I had on her.

"Uh huh, so good" she moaned before I felt her run her tongue up the side of my neck causing me to growl out, my nails digging into her denim shorts as I felt myself getting more and more worked up as her lips and tongue continued to ravish my neck. She was good at this I thought before frowning, why was she so good?

I was about to speak, clearly about to ruin the moment due to me being a jealous and over protective fool when I felt her teeth lightly press against the junction which joined my neck to my shoulder, the action causing me to groan and any words die in my throat as I moved my head to the side so she had more room to work with.

"I would love to meet your parents" I heard her whisper before she was off me, my hands holding air as I gaped her at as she stood there grinning, her face flushed.

"Bloody hell Zoe!" I found myself growling when I realised she had gotten me worked up enough to completely space out only to pull away. She was clearly enjoying my discomfort as I tried to think disgusting thoughts to try and calm down my little problem, my eyes glaring in her direction which only seemed to ignite her laughter as she grinned at me with a wink.

It was then I realised what she had said, my own disgruntled expression turning into a relieved grin as I sprung up to take her into my arms, swinging her around happily as I smiled at her gleeful laughter.

"Thank you" I smiled, knowing how nervous she was when I had first brought it up. I didn't get a reply, only a bright smile and a saucy wink that had me pressing my lips against hers in seconds. I just hoped my parents didn't scare her off since I knew this was going to be my only chance at a first impression when she met my family, the last thing I wanted was for her to want to avoid the pack house where I later wanted her to live with me. So yea...a lot of pressure on my part, so definitely fingers crossed.

Chapter 18

H unter's Pov

Shit.

I couldn't think of anything else to say when I walked into my pack house the following day only to see the two bastards sitting at my table and chatting with my parents as if they hadn't chucked my mate out when she was young! How fucking dare they!

Anger.

Another emotion I felt towards them. Ok that was a fucking understatement. I was raging, furious as I felt my upper lip pull back as I snarled silently, my body shaking with rage as I resisted shifting right there and then and taking them out. What right did they have to sit there? None, they had fucking none after what they did!

I had been walking into the pack house grinning when I glanced at my watch to find she would be here soon, my reason for living. I couldn't believe when she had said yes, I knew she was uncomfortable with it at first but I was relieved when she had said it was ok with her to meet my parents.

Really it had been my parents who had been hinting at me to meet the future alpha-female of the pack, she would receive the title as soon as I had mated and marked her. It was when I caught there scents, the scents I now detested as I entered into the hall only to hear them talking to my parents as if they were the innocents that I had once believed them to be. How could I have been so stupid to think they were good people, they were monsters in my eyes. Lower than some of the vampires I had come across, and that was saying something.

The growls which rumbled in my chest finally caught their attentions as I leaned against the door frame as they sat in the kitchen, my posture stiff and my eyes tinted with my wolfs yellow as I glared at my mates parents who were looking extremely uncomfortable under my gaze. Good.

"Hello dear, what's wrong?" my mother asked panicked as my father immediately scented the surroundings, a habit which he was likely never to drop due to being the previous alpha before I took over my right.

"What are they doing here?" I asked tensely, literally fighting the urge not to give into my instincts and inner wolf which was telling me to shift and rip into their throats. I could picture it now, the taste of blood in my mouth, my wolf purring in pride as I stood in the bloody room. I shook my head rapidly, I could really be disturbed sometimes.

"Oh, you will never guess Hunter. Their daughter is back, you know the one that ran away when she was little. I have no idea what she must have been thinking, I mean leaving a loving family that young" my mother gushed before stopping when she took note of my shaking form, the fact my nails were braking the door frame as I gripped it with inhuman force.

I stared at the pathetic parents in front of me, pure disgust running through me as what Jack had told me continued to run through my head over and over again. I felt sick with anger and pain, the anger being how they treated her and the pain knowing what she must have gone through.

I also couldn't believe the lies they were spreading, hell even gloating. Loving family? A loving family does not kick out there daughter at 12 completely defenceless. A loving family doesn't lie about losing their daughter, the pack spent months trying to track down the small girl only to find she had completely disappeared. What sort of loving family would do something as sick as that? It was disgusting, they were disgusting and apart from Jack I couldn't stand the fucking family!

"Son?" my father's deep voice cut through my mental rage as I snapped my head in his direction only to see him flinch, the fact I was sending out pure alpha vibes and my eyes were most likely my wolfs I knew I wasn't exactly the most friendly face to look at.

"What?" I asked, my voice tight with anger as I continued to glare at the now shying away couple. I couldn't stand them, I hated them and it took a lot for me to purely, instinctively hate someone as much as I did them.

"You need to calm yourself, what has you so worked up?" he asked curiously, following my gaze with confusion as I furiously glared at my mates horrific parents. What kind of childhood did she have? With that thought I suddenly found myself extremely curious to how they treated her before she was kicked out? Were they horrible to her? Did they hit her? That was the thought which made the tremors in my form to rise to a whole new level, if they did then it was my right to seek vengeance against them. Bastards!

"My mate is coming over, I want them gone" I stated, not leaving any room for objections as I stared them down. The fact they were my parents at that moment didn't bother me, only the well-being of my mate was on both mine and my wolfs mind.

"Your mate! Finally I can't wait to meet her-wait why must they leave?" my mother asked, her excited gushing suddenly turning to confusion as to why I wanted the bastards to leave.

"Yes why would we need to leave Hunter, I would love the opportunity to meet the future alpha-female" Lisa stated, the bitch not knowing what she needed to shut her mouth. I glared at the woman who had played a part in my mates sadness, the fact she had put my mate in such a dangerous situation was an unforgiveable act in my eyes. I could also hear the distain hidden in her tone, her jealousy and anger at Stacy not being my mate. Bitch.

"I want you out of this house, right now." I snarled at them, pleased when I saw them flinch away. They were foolish though, staying put and not obeying me like they should have done. I could have alpha ordered them of course, they were in my pack and territory after all, but pain was such a more appealing option at that moment.

"Hunter have some respect, they are good people" My father scolded me, though shocked him when I turned my anger on him for the very first time since I had become the alpha. What right did he have to stand by their side and not mine? How dare he!

"I said I wanted them out, if they refuse then I will physically remove them!" I snapped, my body humming as my muscles twitched with the urge to do just that.

"Now, now why don't we all calm down for a minute. Are you sure this girl is your mate Hunter, I thought you and Stacy were bonding and feeling the mating signals" Peter stated causing me to growl, like I cared what the bastard thought.

"I do not want Stacy. This is your last warning-" I snarled only to be interrupted by my trembling mother. While I didn't like to actually see her fear me, I wasn't in my right frame of mind with these two sitting there, they didn't deserve to be!

"Son please, think of your mate. What would she think of you acting this way?" my father asked, clearly trying to calm me down with thoughts of my mate. Ok I give him that, it was a smart move on his part.

"She would say to get these pathetic excuses of parents out of his fucking house before I rip out their throats myself, and before you ask they wouldn't be the first" a snarl was heard from behind me causing me to tense further at the anger at her tone.

I watched as everyone paled at the sound of her voice, the harshness of her threat and her confession causing the colour to drain from their faces.

You know if she wasn't so pissed off and glaring in my direction, I would have told her she looked as hot as hell when she was as angry. Though I didn't have a death wish, so with my better judgement I kept my lips firmly sealed as my eyes ran over her form with undisguised lust. How the hell was I going to refrain from jumping her when she always looked so damn good?

Chapter 19

H unter's Pov

I cringed when I heard the pure anger in my mates voice, and if I wasn't so focused on how everyone in the room seemed to pale at both her comment and tone I would have taken in how my mates form seemed to tremble before she managed to get a grip of her emotions.

"Everyone this is Zoe, my mate" I introduced as I wrapped an arm around my mates waist, her eyes focused on her parents as pure anger radiated from her every pour. I cringed yet again; this is not how I wanted this meeting to go. I had planned to introduce her to my parents, keep her calm before attempting to approach the topic of her staying the night or moving into a spare room at the least. But I knew that idea was blown out of the water since the last thing I had wanted was for my angel to feel pressured, plus I couldn't exactly approach the subject now since she was looking at me as if it was my fault the idiots were here!

Once Zoe's pathetic excuse of parents finally snapped out of it they plastered fake smiles on their faces, though I could see the wheels turning in their heads as they clearly recognised the girl by my side as the daughter they had made a rouge. If they were any other parents they would be as pleased as hell that there daughter had mated with the alpha, but I could tell from how uneasy they held themselves under our gazes that there past was catching up with them. My eyes held threats and promises; they would suffer to the pits of hell when I was finished with them.

"Urm, hello dear" my mother greeted, sounding as if she was conflicted on whether to feel fear or excitement at meeting Zoe for the first time. She somehow seemed to be feeling both while my father was studying my mate, taking in whether or not he approved that she would soon be the alpha female of the pack. It's not it would stop me seeing and marking her if he said she wasn't good enough for the position, but it would be nice to have his blessing for me to mate with her even if it wouldn't stop me if I didn't.

"Leave" I growled at Zoe's parents, my voice rumbling through-out the pack house as my tone left no room for discussion. The couple quickly left, though not before shooting warning glares in my mates direction causing me to snarl furiously at them, fare to say they ran the rest of the way. It was too late if they expected her not to talk about what they did, I knew thanks to Jack and I would not be forgetting it any time soon that was for sure.

"Fucking bastards" I heard her mutter as she relaxed slightly against me, though she was still tense as she eyed my parents through narrowed eyes. I sighed; this is not how I wanted this to go at all.

"Mum, Dad this is Zoe. Zoe these are my parents Tom and Stella" I introduced as I pulled her towards the table, pulling out her chair as she took a seat. I was as nervous as hell as I raked my fingers through my now messy hair, so much for giving a first good impression I thought bitterly. Yet another thing to hate her parents for, I mean why did they have to arrive back today of all days?

"Hello Zoe, it's nice to finally meet you" My mother greeted as she shuffled further to my father as she did so, obviously worried about my mates reaction.

"It's nice to meet you to, I apologise about my attitude just now but those people are a touchy subject to me" my amazing mate said sweetly, her tone so soft and apologetic that I could immediately see the impact that her words had on my parents. I was stunned before I couldn't help but grin, my mate was truly amazing and I was glad I hadn't fucked up.

"That's fine dear, so why don't you tell us how you met?" My mother continued, leaning forward as she rested her elbows on the table and her chin in her hands, it was clear she was going to try and get every bit of information out of my mate that was possible. I would have been amused if I wasn't worried about how Zoe would take my eager mother, though thankfully she seemed to take it into his stride.

"School actually, he made quite the impression" Zoe stated causing me to stiffen, but one look in her direction was enough for me to see the small smirk tugging at the corner of her mouth. I sighed out relieved, glad that she had seemingly forgiven me and looked past how I had treated her so horribly at the start of the school year. It still hurt me to think about my harsh comments and actions towards her, but I knew I had the rest of our lives to make it up to her.

"That's my boy, so Zoe why don't you tell us about yourself" my father asked, obviously pleased with how she had suddenly turned her attitude around and spoken to my mother with kind and humour filled words.

"Not much to say really. I was kicked out when I was younger so I was forcibly labelled a rouge, I would never had come here if it wasn't for the law" she stated honestly causing me to clench my fists on my lap as I thought back to her past, I still couldn't believe how a parent could do that to a child, especially when the child had clearly done nothing wrong, hell she was 12 for fucks sake!

"Oh my" my mother gasped, slapping her hand over her mouth as she gazed at my mate in a whole new light. I could practically see the sympathy and pity rolling off my mother, my father quick to comfort her but I could tell he was just as horrified by her comment as my mother was.

"Well I am glad we have none of that in our pack" my father stated causing me to internally wince, if only he knew it had in fact happened right under his nose when he was the running alpha. I was actually looking forward to that conversation, knowing I wouldn't be the only one out for blood when it all came out. He had after all issued searches for my mate when the news got around, hell the family was fussed around by the pack due to their apparent loss! They had milked the attention for all it was worth, the thought sickened me.

The rest of the day was thankfully not as dramatic as it was at the start, the bastards not coming back and my parents getting alone with Zoe like a house on fire. It wasn't until it was time for Zoe to head home that I found my whole body protesting, wanting her to stay and not to leave me yet.

"I should be making a move, it's getting late" she seemed to sigh reluctantly, and while it warmed me that she didn't seem to want to leave me as much as I didn't want to part from her I still didn't want her to leave.

"Already? Why don't we watch a film?" I asked, panicking slightly since neither me nor my wolf wanted her to leave just yet. The rest of the pack had arrived hours ago, in their rooms with their mates as I sat in the living room with Zoe who was currently curled up at my side. I had never been more comfortable then I was now.

"I don't know-"

"Please" I breathed, my tone filled with hope and longing. I didn't care if I sounded pathetic, as long as she stayed then the desperate vibe I gave off was worth it.

I watched as she seemed to considered it, her emerald eyes running over my features before she sighed and relaxed back against me. I grinned; I couldn't help it as she rolled her head to the side to look at me, her dark locks sprawling over the back of the couch as she locked her eyes with mine.

"Fine, put something on then" she sighed with a smile causing me to grin, my arms having a mind of their own as they wrapped around her waist and pulled her onto my lap, her squeal of laughter and surprize causing me to grin as her laughter filled the room as I tickled her sides.

I couldn't help but smile as her laughter filled the room, and while her body wiggling and rubbing against mine only fuelled my urge to claim her I tried to push past it as I concentrated on the adorable giggles which spilled from her curved lips as her eyes shined with mirth and humour.

"You're beautiful" I found myself saying as I laid her on the couch, straddling her hips as I leaned over her panting and flushed form, my nose nearly brushing hers with how close I was. I didn't mean for the comment to slip out, but I couldn't help but be honest with her and that was exactly what she was. She was beautiful, so beautiful.

"You're not so bad yourself handsome" she winked, her hand raising as her fingers brushed a strand of my dark hair as it fell over my eyes slightly. I needed a hair-cut, but as she tugged on a strand I couldn't help the groan which came with her action.

"Uh huh" I replied; only partly paying attention as she continued to play and tug at the strand of dark hair.

"Come on, put a film on" she whined playfully as she gave it one last tug before pushing me off her, my back connecting with the floor causing me to grunt out in annoyance and surprize.

"You seem to manhandle me more and more each day" I muttered as I sat up with a scowl, looking in her direction only for my lips to turn into a smile when I saw her. Her hand was over her mouth as she tried to muffle her laughter, her face flushed and her eyes bright with amusement. She was a vision.

"You love it" she grinned once she had calmed down, sprawling out of the couch as she watched me grab a DVD before crouching down to put it in the DVD player. She had told me she liked horrors in one of our chats so I specifically choose one for her to watch, not to mention horror was my favourite genre as well.

"That I do" I muttered. It may have only been weeks but I knew I was already falling for her, hard, and I found I didn't mind that I was one bit.

Chapter 20

Hunters Pov

When I woke up I felt my eyelids heavy with the remains of sleep, the fact I had yet to wake up fully sinking into my mind as I groaned at the streak of sunlight which had managed to sneak past my thick curtains as it shone on my face much to my dis-enjoyment.

Making a move to shift I stiffened when I suddenly became extremely aware of the hot skin which was pressed against mine, my eyes finally opening slightly as I looked down only to be greeted with the raven coloured locks as they sprawled out on my bare chest.

I knew I would have panicked that it was some random girl if it wasn't for the signs which pointed that the gorgeous and still sleeping girl was in fact my adorable and edible mate. The fact it was the best night's sleep of my life, how my wolf was so content, so satisfied that I felt as if I was on top of the world. Not to mention the way her body fitted perfectly with mine as if she had been made for me only, how her skin touching mine elicited a delightful and addicting feeling which I had begun to crave since the moment we had first touched.

Smiling down at her I was suddenly all too aware that all she was only wearing one of my shirts and her undergarments, both of us getting distracted with watching a number of films before we both realised that it was dark outside and already past midnight. I had refused to let her go home when it was so late, so she had relented and stayed.

I wasn't complaining, far from it since her being in my bed with me was more than I had expected. Sure I hadn't claimed her, we had actually been on separate sides of the bed until I woke up to find my arm around her waist, her head on my chest and our legs entwined as we sprawled out on my large bed. No, I wasn't complaining at all.

Sighing I brought her closer against me, greedily socking up the time and contact I had with her before she made her excuses and left. I didn't like the fact she still seemed to distance herself from me, but I knew it would take time to let her trust me fully and I knew once I had it there was no way I was going to let it go. She was my everything.

Grinning like a cat that got the cream I let my fingers trail along the skin of her arm, feeling the addicting sparks which made both me and my wolf purr in delight. God she felt amazing, amazing being an understatement.

"Mm..."

Hearing her moan I immediately felt myself getting aroused by the sensual sound which passed her plump lips, her body pressing closer against mine as I felt her warm breath on the skin of my chest making me shiver.

"Shit" I muttered before craning my neck to look at the time, my eyes widening slightly before narrowing when I realised we would have to leave for school soon.

As soon as the thought passed through my mind I heard footsteps heading in the direction of my room causing my eyes to narrow even more so before my voice rumbled towards the direction I knew to be Collin, my beta.

"Don't open the door, leave without me" I stated under my breath, not wanting to wake up Zoe but not wanting to leave. Frowning when I felt her shift in my grasp I heard Collin reply before the front door shut, everyone clearly already leaving for school.

I knew skipping school wasn't the best and most moral thing to do but if it was between spending the day at school or with my edible and amazing mate then what would you choose? Exactly, so my mate it is.

It was just under an hour later I felt her start to stir, the fact I had been doing nothing but gazing at her since I had woken shocking me slightly since it felt as if no time at all had passed. I found I loved watching her sleep, it being a creepy Edward Cullen move but I found it didn't bother me. She was a light sleeper I found, even the slightest noise in my room causing her to stir lightly before nodding back off to sleep.

"Hunter" she breathed as she pressed herself further against me, the fact I wanted nothing more than to rip my shirt off her and ravish her until she couldn't remember her own name as she screamed mine not helping with me trying to calm my urges to jump and mound her right there and then.

"Wake up baby" I breathed sensually in her ear, feeling her shiver against me as I did so.

I watched grinning when she pulled out of my grip as she sat up, her hands clenching in small fists as she tried to rub the sleep from her eyes. She looked so adorably cute, she was all his!

"Hunter?" her soft and sleepy voice filled the room causing my already large grin to widen, I couldn't help it! She was just....so cute.

"Morning baby, how'd you sleep?" I asked as I pushed a strand of her dark and slightly mattered locks behind her ear before cupping her face in my palm, so pretty and delicate.

"Fine, what's the time?" she asked and I could tell she was still half asleep. This was the part I was slightly nervous about, her reaction to me not waking her when it was time for school. The conversation could go both ways, she could accept it or she could be more than annoyed with me, a reaction which I was not hoping for.

"10:30" I stated with a wince, expecting some sort of reaction from her about missing school. I was shocked when I got none though, her expression slightly amused as a small smile tugged at the corner of her lips as she let her back hit the mattress of the bed, her hair splayed out across the pillow making her look nothing short of an angel.

"10:30 huh? Take it no school for us then" she winked, her eyes sparking in a way which filled me with warmth knowing I had made her happy.

"Nope, I must admit though I thought you would be more than a little pissed at me" I confessed with a wince, not knowing how to understand her reaction.

"Pissed at you for what?" she asked curiously as she propped herself up on her elbow, her hair tumbling over her shoulders in uneven curls. I couldn't help but think she still looked incredibly beautiful to me though, so beautiful.

"You know, not waking you up for school, wanting you all to myself" I trailed off as I pulled the sheet away from her from to drink in the slight of her in my light blue button up shirt, seeing her roll her eyes but not commenting as my eyes continued to greedily drink in the sight in front of me.

"I don't mind, deciding between spending time with you or going to school isn't exactly a difficult decision now is it?" she winked, leaning forward to press her lips gently to mine before hopping off the bed and heading into my bathroom before I could even think of pulling her closer to me. Fuck, I was so whipped.

Chapter 21

- -

Zoe's Pov

I couldn't help but grin as I sprinted into the bathroom, the fact he was being so sweet meaning that he was successfully breaking down my inner walls that I had spent years putting up with effectively little ease. I didn't really know what to think of it, but I knew I could and would be extremely happy if I let him in and I was slowly doing so, but I knew I needed time.

When he stuck up for me when my pathetic parents were in the kitchen when I arrived I couldn't help but feel touched, even when I was blind with rage that he had the bastards in his house I couldn't help but let my gaze soften when I looked at him. I knew I may have overreacted with my comment, but what I said was nothing short of true since I had ripped out a number of throats in my past due to being a rouge, just because I was mated to an alpha didn't change that fact at all.

I couldn't believe have close I had been to phrasing right there and then when I caught both there familiar scent and spotted them sitting at the table as if they hadn't abandoned a child who had been merely 12, the tremors raking through my body as I tried to hold off on the urge to become one with my wolf when I caught sight of them. I had never had so much trouble calming my urges before, but then again I never expected to meet the people that made my life hell again and not to attack with the intent to kill instantly.

I had always pictured what it would be like if I met them again, let's just say it involved screams, blood and me cackling sadistically as I looked at their bloody and still bodies. Depressing I know, but one can dream.

Quickly taking a shower I slipped back on my bra as well as the shirt I had 'borrowed' from Hunter before frowning at what to wear under the shirt, while at home it wouldn't have bothered me I didn't exactly want Hunter to catch a glimpse of me going commando. I trusted him with asking him to take it slow, but I knew he only had so much restraint.

Sighing I looked around the room before grabbing a pair of clean boxers which he had piled on a shelf, slipping them on before rolling the waist band over a few times since there were massive on my small form.

"Perfect" I beamed before glancing at my reflection, grabbing his comb which lay on the sink before struggling to brush my hair with it. Couldn't he use a brush like normal people?

Once I was sure I looked fine I walked back into the bedroom only to freeze when a growl suddenly filtered into my ears, the sound making me shiver in delight as I slowly turned around only to shudder when I caught sight of what was in front of me. There Hunter was, shirtless in only a pair of boxers, looking at me as if I was a gazelle and he was the lion.

I couldn't help but find it arousing, who wouldn't when your hot as hell mate was looking at you like you were his prey. His eyes were dark, almost a pitch black instead of their normal hazel brown as his gaze raked over my form in a way which made me feel as if I was naked and bare in front of him.

His nostrils were flaring, obviously picking up on how suddenly heated I felt under his gaze. I knew he could smell my arousal, and for some reason that only served as a further turn on for me. YUM!

It was when my eyes ran over his body that I felt myself nearly combust with desire, want and lust. His own lust was clearly visible from the dent in his boxers, and I had to literally snap my head back to his to prevent drooling over his more than adequate bulge.

My head was becoming hazy with pleasure, I was so out of it that I didn't hear nor see Hunter move until he was in front of me, a deep and constant growl rumbling in his chest as he looked down on me. He practically towered over my from, making me seem more than a little petite compared to his height as I had to crane my head up slightly to look into his dark and lustful gaze. Oh god did I want him...

"Zoe" was all he growled, and as if reading my thoughts he pinned me against the wall in seconds, his lips crashing onto mine in a fierce dance as we fought for dominance. He didn't bother to ask permission for his tongue to enter my mouth, no he forced it passed my lips so roughly and quickly that I felt my toes curl on his dark carpet as I moaned into his mouth.

"God, what are you doing to me?" he grunted in my neck as well pulled apart, somehow my legs had wrapped themselves around his waist as I ground against him with more than a little passion. I knew if he wasn't holding back, fearing that he would push me too far, he would have taken me right there and then against the wall. It was that thought I knew he was perfect, I mean who many guys would be sweet and caring enough to wait?

Knowing I needed to slow this down, and while the last thing I would mind was pouncing on him right there and then I wasn't ready for him marking me. I knew the urge would be too much for him to resist while we mated, his teeth sinking into where my throat joined my neck as soon as we climaxed and I wasn't ready to be tied down so much yet. I knew we would eventually end up together, hopefully, but I didn't want it to be labelled yet and I would be if I let him. I was not ready to be the alpha female, far from it due to being so used to being alone for so many years.

Slowing down the kiss I stopped it by playing with his bottom lip in my mouth, nipping it slightly before releasing it with a lustful grin. We were both still panting, his hands firmly on my upper thighs as he held me against the wall. Sighing I took in his flushed and aroused state, I had never seen anything sexier.

"What was that for?" I panted with a lustful grin, squeezing at his shoulders to get him to put me down. He did so, though I could feel the pure reluctance and effort it took him to step a few paces away from me. I would have felt guilty, if I wasn't feeling the exact same.

"I like you in my clothes" was all he said before practically running into the bathroom, leaving me grinning when I heard the shower turn on.

"Cold shower it is then" I smirked, speaking my amused thoughts out loud as I shook my head with a chuckle. Though the mental image of him standing naked, water running down his body and abs was enough to snap me out of it as I practically bolted out the door as to not be tempted to join him...

Chapter 22

Hunter's Pov

It had been a few weeks since Zoe had stayed round and I was pleased to note that it wasn't the last, and while things didn't get as heated I was content and happy with her presence alone. If she wanted to wait that was fine by me, her presence was enough even if my wolf didn't think so.

Today happened to be one of the days in which Zoe didn't sleep around and I had to suffer through waking up alone, surrounded by her delicious and vibrant scent which only made me miss her further. Since that night she had stayed when it was too late for her to go home I couldn't sleep right without her, I felt out of place and constantly tense unless I was pressed up against her, her head on my chest or our legs entwined. She was my soul-mate, my other half so it didn't come to a surprize that I felt like half of me was missing when she wasn't around.

Saying that though things had been going great, and though I haven't brought up the issue with her parents she knew I was aware that she didn't run away. She hadn't asked me straight out, but it was clear from how I loathed them that she had put two and two together. That was what Jack had been worried about, her reaction to him spilling the beans, even if he couldn't help himself due to being unable to fight an Alpha order. She didn't seem to mind though, but I knew she was hiding something just not what.

Sighing I rubbed my face roughly before getting ready for school, eager to see Zoe again. I couldn't wait to look into those gorgeous emerald eyes of hers, run my fingers through her mane of dark curls or pull her against me. It was my idea of pure and utter heaven.

Grabbing my bag once I was ready to go, my hair still wet from my shower I took the steps two at a time as I pounded down the stairs and into the kitchen. I took note of the members of my pack that were in there, unfortunately Stacy happened to be present as well.

She had thankfully been keeping her distance since the whole lunch hall incident, the fact she had blamed my mate in front of the entire pack meaning that most were avoiding her more than usual. It's not like I blamed them, hell the only reason guys hung around with her was because she was easy.

"Hunter baby, morning"

I raised a brow at her unimpressed, Ellie and Hannah glaring from their mates sides as she did so. Everyone had become fiercely protective over Zoe, even Josh who had hated rouges with a passion enjoyed her dry humour and company to the point he actually asked when she was coming round. Hannah had been incredibly pleased with his sudden change of attitude, the sex ban he had told me had been lifted. He was pleased to say the least.

"I am not your baby Stacy, so stop with the names!" I snapped, I did not want her doing that shit when Zoe was around. The last thing I needed was more problems from the slag, she was on thin ice as it was.

"When will you realise that we are mates Hunter! That....bitch of a sister of mine is nothing, you're just confused" she whined, growling filling the room as soon as she dared to insult my mate. Did she have a death wish, hopefully she did.

Dropping my bag by the door I stormed over towards her, I knew my eyes were most likely my wolves as my hand wrapped around her scrawny neck as my grip tightened just enough to make her feel it.

"We are not mates! We will never be mates and for that I am fucking glad! But you dare insult Zoe again and I will rip you apart, are we clear?" I snapped at her, my tone filled with anger and authority as my body trembled with the attempt not to phase right there and then and end her once and for all. Unfortunately I couldn't act at the moment, but it wouldn't be long until I managed to get rid of the bitch.

Her eyes had gone comically wide as soon as I had started storming over, fear and panic flashing through her gaze when she realised that insulting Zoe may not have been the best thing to do, especially in mine and the packs presence.

"I...uh..." was all she managed to gurgle out, my eyes rolling when she tried to claw at my hand to try and get me to release my grip. I released it slightly, though kept her in a firm grip as I leaned forward so my gaze was burning into hers, the scent of her perfume burning my nose slightly as I did so. Wasn't having a strong sense of smell enough without having to flood the place with that aroma she called perfume?

"Are we clear?" I snapped, vaguely aware of everyone's eyes on me but like I expected no one commented or even tried to interfere in my rough treatment of Stacy. Honestly nobody cared, I mean who was stupid enough to insult the alphas mate?

"I'm your...mate" she stupidly tried to get out, my grip tightening again as she tried to struggle against me as I picked her off the ground so her toes barely skimmed the wooden floor.

"Are we clear?" I tried again, feeling her try to nod before I released her abruptly from my grip causing her to stumble when she tried to regain her balance by gripping the counter. She was breathing heavily, trying to refill her burning lungs but again it didn't bother me in the slightest. It was her own fault, she needed to learn the hard way.

It was Jack who broke the tension, Stacy glaring accusing at Jack as if he would interfere with an alpha to protect the so called sister who treated him like shit much like his parents when he pledged his loyalty to me after deciding that the last thing he wanted was to be Alpha. Not only didn't he stand a chance fighting against me, but he didn't want the responsibility which came with it. It was understandable

I suppose, I could see where he was coming from but I loved being Alpha and nothing would change that for me.

"Good for you mate, bitch needs to learn a lesson" he stated as if Stacy wasn't his sister, snorts of amusement coming from the guys as giggles and sniggers escaped the females of the pack. I couldn't help but roll my eyes, trying to fight a grin as I did so.

"Jack! Why didn't you help me?" Stacy just had to whine, her voice slightly croaky due to my assault on her neck. I could already see the bruises I caused healing rapidly though, they would be gone in a few minutes at the most. While she was a female shifter unfortunately, she was strangely a slow healer for a shifter but we had pegged it down to all female shifters being that way, we didn't have anyone else to compare it to.

"Me, help you Stacy? Why would I do that?" Jack asked with a raised brow, grinning as his head snapped to the door as Chloe came bouncing in with a shy smile we had all come to know and love on her.

"I am your sister!" she screeched before wincing, Chloe flinching at the harsh tone causing Jack to become even more pissed with his sister. They didn't get on well, but now she had upset his mate I could see the anger which flashed through his gaze as he pushed Chloe behind him slightly.

"Only by blood, but Stacy you are no sister of mine!" he snapped, Chloe rubbing his shoulders soothingly causing everyone in the pack to grin. She was a naturally shy person, but when it came to Jack she seemed to come out of her shell more.

"I'm telling dad!" she cried out. I was actually surprised his comment seemed to hit her hard, her eyes glossing over but again no one made a mood to comfort her. She had dug her own grave and nobody wanted to lie with her in it.

"Whatever Stacy" Jack muttered frowning, pulling Chloe against him as he breathed in her scent to relax him. It was clear her comment had upset him, and I didn't like it.

"Right get your stuff and get out" I stated as I walked to grab my bag, her eyes widening comically as she gaped at me.

"What?" she gaped, obviously thinking I was kicking her out. It was in my right to do so, but unfortunately it wasn't the right time. Her parents were staying at my own parents house while there house was getting fixed and I didn't want my parents to have to put up with another selfish brat.

"Get to school! I am not your fucking father Stacy but I am your alpha, you do not treat my closest friends like shit in MY pack!" I snapped at her, getting in her face as I grabbed her wrist as pulled her towards the door. I may have sounded harsh, but she needed some touch love to grow the fuck up!

"It's our pack" she corrected me, everyone gaping at her in disbelief. Did she really believe she was welcome here, she was hated!

"It is not your pack Stacy, it is MINE! And while you are in my territory you are under my ruling and authority, if you don't like it then leave!" I snapped, trying to hide a smile when I took note of how Ellie's eyes light up as Collin pinched her thigh slightly in a playful manner but gave me a nod of respect, clearly agreeing with me.

I watched as Stacy seemed to want to say something else but thinking better of it, clearing she had some self-preservation then.

"Fine" she stated before spinning on her heel and storming out the door, going to her car as she headed to school on her own. Her parents had brought her own car for her, and while there was a pack account due to not all of my pack members coming from well off families she didn't have a card to access it. That did remind me to get one done in Zoe's name though, I knew she didn't have a lot to her name but she had done incredibly well for a rouge.

"Fucking bitch" I muttered as I swung my bag over my shoulder before heading out the door, giving a short wave to everyone as they headed to their own cars and pulled out behind me.

Reaching the school I quickly made my way inside, glancing down at my watch only to sigh when I saw I was at least twenty minutes late for my first lesson. I hadn't realised my argument with Stacy had lasted so long, but she needed to be put in her place!

Quickly heading inside I suddenly found myself frowning when I couldn't sense Zoe inside. Even though we had yet to mate I could still tell when she was close, and I was extremely aware that she wasn't in the school like she expected.

Walking over to the reception I immediately caught the attention of the receptionist, her eyes widening as she quickly sat up straighter. I could practically sense the nervousness coming off her in waves and I knew she would be calling her mate as soon as I left, he would be able to have a firm grip on her emotions after all and would worry.

"Alpha...sir, what can I do for you?" she asked instantly when I approached, clearly hoping that she had done nothing to bring on my temper. I wanted to roll my eyes, but I was far too interested in my mate whereabouts to bother with the action.

"Is my mate here?" I asked, already knowing she wasn't but wanting to know if she had signed in before wondering off somewhere. If she had then she would be back soon, that was what I was hoping and counting on.

The receptionist started typing away at her keyboard without delay as her eyes quickly ran over the screens monitor, my fingers thumping on the wooden desk which I doubted helped her with her nerves. It was instinct to feel nervous around your alpha, it was one of the reasons I had so much power over my pack.

"She hasn't signed in Sir" she muttered nervously, my nails digging into the wood causing her to jump away from me slightly.

"Thank you" I stated before walking off, grabbing my phone from my pocket before quickly flicking through it to find her number. Where the fuck was she?

Chapter 23

- -

Zoe's Pov

I ignored my phone as it went off, my hands clenched into fists as my upper lip pulled back into a silent snarl. I could feel my palms dampening, my nails cutting deep into my flesh hard enough for me to bleed. I couldn't help but laugh out bitterly, the bastards who stood in front of me flinching away due to the harshness of my laughter as I glared at them furiously.

How. Dare. They!

"What?" I spat, my voice filled with venom as I tried to calm myself from attacking them right there and then. I certainly wouldn't regret it, plus I knew it would be so worth it to hear their screams of pain as I ripped them apart. No, I would enjoy every single second of it.

"We want you to leave" yep, that was what I thought they said. Could you believe the cheek they had on them, to not only approach me when I was walking down the street but to actually think they had any claim over me to think they could tell me what to do? Oh hell no…I would rather die than have anything to do with them again!

"What makes you think I would listen to you?" I snapped out, pleasure filling me when I saw them try to be subtle as they edged away from my slightly trembling form. That's right, you should be scared of me!

"We are your parents?" my dick of a father spat causing my eyes to widen at the nerve the man had, he seriously didn't just say that did he?

"You are no father of mine! You are a dirty old man who finds pleasure in beating the shit out of children!" I snarled, his laughs and cackles haunting me as I remembered how he would beat me only to laugh when I would cry. I was a child for fucks sake and he beat the shit out of me just for the hell of it! Who in their right mind could do that to a child!?

"I do not!" he had the nerve to lie to my face, my anger continuing to rise as he did so.

"No? So when you would whip me with your belt until my back split I was imagining it? When you would shove me down the stairs you were playing? When you repeatedly made me feel unworthy, be your slave, smack me around you were being a good father!" I screamed at him, seeing them stumble back as I did so. I couldn't help but want to rip them apart, they disgusted me!

"Don't speak to him like that, whether you like it or not you are our child you ungrateful brat" oh, so my bitch of a mother speaks.

"You lost the right to call me your daughter when you tossed me away at the age of 12" I hissed lowly, seeing their own anger rise and I knew if they didn't fear me they would have most likely attacked me already. I was messing with their plans, they wanted Stacy to mate with Hunter and to gain the benefits which came with it.

"You will listen to us Zoe" he threatened, it was pathetic.

"Or what?" I challenged as I stepped forward, getting in his face. I had nothing to lose apart from Hunter and he can bloody look after himself.

"Or we will end you" he threatened causing me to scoff. See what sort of a family I had been born into, it was disgusting to think people like these were allowed to have kids. They were horrible people who deserved none of the things they had, bastards!

"Are you threatening me?" I asked with an amused laugh, hell they were afraid of me when they didn't know I could shift, they would probably have fainted if they were aware of all the facts. Not that I would be telling them anytime soon, it's not like I had even the smallest amount of trust in them.

"Yes, but not just you Zoe" my bitch of a mother stated smugly, her tone making me look at her in revolution. She didn't deserve to have kids, neither of them did.

"Oh no?" I taunted, who could they hold over me exactly.

"We may not want to lose our son Zoe, but Chloe is a whole other story" she threatened causing my eyes to widen, oh fuck no!

Chapter 24

Zoe's Pov

I wanted to kill them, I wanted to rip them apart and bathe in their blood for what my bitch of a mother had the nerve to threaten me with. What kind parents were they? Just because Jack wasn't stupid enough to try and fight Hunter for the alpha position did that mean they no longer want him? That much like myself they wanted to cast him away with nothing but a flick of their wrists? The fact that they had threatened not only a sweet girl such as Chloe, but the fact that she was Jack's mate was horrific and disgusting!

So yea, I wanted them dead but could you blame me? They were nothing, no they were worse than nothing due to the fact we were flesh and blood and as I watched them retreat due to my harsh and clearly frightening gaze I knew they realised they had made a mistake. You do not threaten a rouge, unless you had a death wish that is.

"What. Did. You. Say?" I asked, making sure I said each and every word with both venom and force. I so much wanted to phase and kill them, but I couldn't handle the bullshit that was bound to come after it. No-one knew but Jack what my family had done to me and by killing them I would have them after me for revenge. It was a shame really, how the pack didn't realise what sort of people they were protecting.

I watched pleased as they flinched away from me, it was hardly surprising but again I was pleased with their response to my words. They knew I didn't care for them, they knew it wouldn't bother me if they died and the fact I was a rogue only added to the fear which was slowly mounting on them. They may have thought I couldn't shift, but even a female without the ability could inflict some serious pain.

"Nothing..." my bitch of a mother whimpered, she had tried to come off brave but the fact she was shaking like a leaf meant it wasn't possible for her to do so. Good.

"No, you said something and I want you to repeat it. So come on, spit it out!" I snapped at them, wanting them to say it again so I could have more of a reason to plan my killing of them. I was a patient person, I think I could live with planning how to make it look like an accident – even if it took a little longer than I would have liked. Yep, I liked that idea very much.

I gazed at them through a rage filled haze as they tried to subtly move away, they knew they couldn't attack even if they wanted to. Whether they liked it or not I was the Alphas mate, so he would feel me in pain if they tried anything and even though we had yet to claim and mark each other if he felt my pain he would be able to track me, to be honest I didn't want him here at the moment however harsh that may have seemed.

"We...urm..."

"Spit it out!" I snarled, sick of both this and their company. I had woken up this morning in a good mood which had completely been wreaked thanks to the bastards who shook in front of me, what was wrong with them? Were they sad enough to wait long enough to spot me only to start shouting when they had noticed me walking past? Yes, it was clear they were but I doubt they realised they were never hidden from me to begin with; I could smell them from miles away from where they had hidden.

"I said if you didn't leave our alpha alone we would take care of Chloe" my mother rushed out causing me to look at her in disgust, I didn't think it was possible for me to think any less of them until she had come out with that comment. It was sickening; Chloe was a sweet and shy hearted girl who didn't deserve this threat! I may not know her very well yet, but whether she knew it or not she had my protection simply because she was good to my brother.

"Are you now?" I sneered, having to close my eyes briefly so I didn't alert Hunter to my strong feelings. I didn't need his panicking, and the fact I had turned my phone off as soon as he had called was a sure sign that he was going to have my arse when I saw him next.

"Not if you-"

"NO! You listen to this; I will only be saying it once. Chloe as well as any member of the pack you have seen me with is under my protection, you hurt them and I will make sure that by the time I am finished with you there will be nothing left for them to identify your bodies with! Is that clear?" I pretty much screamed at them, startled and fearful yelps falling from their lips as they nodded quickly. I knew they didn't even think it through though; they were cowardly enough to think that I would believe them when they nodded obediently. I didn't, like I trusted them enough to do so.

With that I spun on my heel and stormed towards the school, tempted to skip but I didn't want to worry Hunter more. I knew he would be concerned and angry, but to be honest the thought of curling up on his lap was too much to resist in that moment and if I had to listen to his shouting then I would rather do so while enjoying his presence. So yep, school it was.

Chapter 25

Zoe's Pov

Walking into the large building also known as school I sighed as I headed towards the receptionist who looked like she was on the phone trying to calm someone down. Her brows were pulled together in a large frown as she tried to calm down who I guessed to be her mate on the other end of the call. Apparently he had felt a large wave of fear come from her and wanted to see her in person to check that she was in fact alright like she had said, only for the woman to say it was unnecessary. I knew it was rude for me to listen in on the clearly private call, but I couldn't help but search for anything that would help to lighten my mood.

Approaching her I leaned against the counter as I waited for her to finish talking to her mate, I wasn't in any rush due to it only being about 10 minutes until the lunch bell would ring so I didn't interrupt. So with that I casually leaned against the wooden counter as my nails tapped gently against the wood, she was to into her conversation to notice me until about 5 minutes later when she let loose a startled but relieved yelp when she saw me.

"Honey I have to go...everything is fine yes, I called you later...love you" she quickly rushed into the phone before hanging up, my brows raising at how suddenly relieved she looked when she spotted me. What was going on?

"Hey, I need to sign in" I commented as I bit my lip, suddenly finding myself starved. I hadn't eaten breakfast since I didn't have any food in my apartment; I really needed to find a job I thought with a frown. It's not like I had anything against working, truthfully when I wasn't hunting and surviving in animal form I was working as much as possible to earn a living. So no it didn't bother me, but I knew it would mean I would have less time with my mate which truthfully didn't sit well with me. I liked my time with Hunter: I didn't want to have to give it up to work.

"Zoe right?" The receptionist asked hopefully, my brows rising at the relief in her tone. What the hell was she on? I barely knew the woman and yet she was relieved to see me? Weirdo!

"Yep" I smiled, watching her grin suddenly before the irritating sound of her fingers on the computer keys filled my sensitive hearing, my mood still agitated but at least the pull in my chest had lessened a little due to me being closer to my mate. I knew he would be pissed, but it would be worth having to listen to him shout at me if I could curl up on his lap while he did it. To be honest I just wasn't in the mood, still finding myself angered at my disgusting parents who had the nerve to threaten not only me but my brother's mate. They would pay, I just needed to bide my time.

"Alright your signed in, try and be on time next time" she asked almost cautiously, clearly not wanting to upset me with her suggestion that my timing wasn't the best. Rolling my eyes I gave her a dramatic nod before heading towards the canteen, the bell going just as I reached the hall. Talk about perfect timing!

As soon as I entered the canteen I took note of the few students already sitting in there, clearly either having skipped classes or having been told that they could work somewhere other than in the classroom. We didn't always have to sit in a class when we worked, since if all we were doing was looking over notes or revising then we could do it about anywhere as long as we were working and out of the way of other students so we didn't disturb them. I preferred to do it outside, my wolf calm due to the nature in addition to the fact I liked being surrounded by both trees and flowers. I found it both relaxing and beautiful!

Grinning in relief I immediately headed to grab some food, choosing a banana milkshake and a ham roll as I did so. I was on a budget after all, it wasn't like I could go all out like most people and to be honest I was already pushing my limit already by getting a drink as well.

Heading to where I normally sat with the guys I took my usual seat before instantly tucking into my food, trying to slow down to savour the taste but finding it almost impossible to do so. I was just about finished when everyone else started coming in, my wolf purring as the ache in my chest grew weaker and weaker as my hunk of a mate grew closer. I knew to prepare myself for a lashing but I couldn't help but grin as I saw him enter, pouting slightly when I saw his eyes narrow in both annoyance and relief at seeing me sitting here.

"Where were you?" he immediately asked as soon as he was in what he thought to be my hearing range, when I could have heard him from the other side of the canteen as clearly as he would have heard me. I stifled rolling my eyes, having to remind myself that I had yet to tell him that I was more than just a female wolf but a shifter. I was not looking forward to that conversation, at all.

"Sorry I got....distracted" I cringed, thinking back to the conversation I had previously that day. I still couldn't believe the nerve they had, what the hell was wrong with the idiots? Did they not have any self-preservation?

"Why?" he instantly asked, clearly wanting to know what had upset me. I smiled; I couldn't help but let my eyes soften as they usually did when he was being so sweet.

"Don't worry about it, it's been dealt with" I waved it off, not wanting to get into it but by the look on his face it was clear that he wouldn't be letting it go like I wished he would. Sighing I nodded, silently telling him that I would explain some other time which would hopefully never come up. I had ways of making him forget my lustful side purred, though I had to admit it did sound more than a little tempting.

"I'll be back in a second" he quickly stated after a few minutes, pressing his lips to mine briefly before heading to grab some food with the rest of the pack, my eyes sorting out Ellie as she sat next to me while Collin went to get her lunch.

"Well he handled that better than I thought" I heard her grin amused, though I could tell much like myself she was stunned at how calmly he had approached me. Hell I had been expecting him to flip out, but again he had managed to make my stomach flutter and my heart to skip a beat due to him being so sweet. He really was breaking down my inner walls quickly, even though they had taken me years to build them up.

"You're not the only one" I muttered as I grabbed my drink and ripped open the annoying little packed that held my straw, stabbing it into my carton before I took a long sip. Moaning I couldn't help but wink when I heard Ellie laugh at my heavenly expression, I couldn't help it, banana milkshake was my weakness.

"So are you going to tell him what had you coming in late, he had been out of his mind when you hadn't turned up this morning?" she asked curiously, not being noisy which I was thankful for. She hadn't asked me what had happened which was a relief, she had only asked if I was going to tell Hunter. Did I tell you that I loved this girl?

"Collin is a lucky boy" was all I winked causing her to laugh out loud, her giggles causing a purr to come from Collins chest as he approached his mate grinning while he handed her the food he had brought for her.

"That I can agree with Zoe" he grinned as he kissed Ellie on the cheek and pulled her close, a 'aw' coming from my mouth causing him to flush slightly which was even cuter. He was just adorable!

"I hope you're not trying to steal my mate Collin, the last thing I need is competition" Hunter joked as he came up behind me, pulling me out of my seat only for me to find myself soon situated in his lap causing me to roll my eyes but grin his way.

"He has nothing on you babe" I winked causing him to growl playfully, the sound going straight to the appendix between my thighs as he did so. Why did he have to sound so hot when he growled? It always made me shiver in delight, knowing this he only seemed to growl at every opportunity just to wind me up. He was a jerk! But he was my jerk!

"Good" he smirked, shooting a mock triumphant look in Collin's direction who only rolled his eyes at his Alphas childishness as the rest of the pack laughed at the playful banter. "Because your mine" he growled huskily in my ear, the scent of my arousal at his tone catching his attention as he groaned against my shoulder. His grip on me tightened as I felt the evidence of his own excitement in the form of a delicious bulge which I had the pleasure of sitting on. YUM!

"Keep it in the bedroom guys!" Josh smirked clearly intending to make me flush in embarrassment. I smirked back, sorry mate but it had nothing to feel embarrassed about, I was more than happy to know how I seemed to affect my mate so strongly. I knew I couldn't hold off much longer, both my body and my wolf were craving to mate fully with him and I had no idea how he was managing to hold back until I was ready, he was not only a male wolf but he was the alpha which only increased his need to claim an alpha female. I loved him even more that he was actually cared enough about my feelings not to try and pressure me into anything that I wasn't ready for. He was perfect!

Rolling my eyes the table soon relaxed into playful banter, laughs and jokes flowing around the table as at one point Hannah and Kelly were laughing so hard at something me and Ellie had joked about that if it hadn't of been for their mates sitting next to them then they would have fallen off the table due to them laughing so hard.

"I'll be back in a sec" Hunter breathed in my ear causing me to nod while I was listening to a dirty joke Josh was telling me, the boy having such a perverted mind that I couldn't help but laugh at the embarrassed look on Hannah's face as she listened to her mate talk animatedly about a joke that was far from being PG.

Giving Hunter my empty milk carton since I had already finished my drink a while ago he moved to throw it into the bin as I hopped off his lap, already missing his presence as he headed over to the line queuing for food. He didn't take long, back in seconds as he held a few items in his right hand, his other being put to good loose as he picked me up and re-positioned me back on his lap as soon as he had returned.

"Here you go, baby" he purred as he held out a yellow carton for me, my eyes lighting up as I pulled his lips to mine as I held onto his cheeks to keep him in place. I couldn't help but thrust my tongue into his mouth in thanks, his grip tightening on me as he moaned into my mouth, drawing a gasp from my own as I soon found his tongue caressing mine in a way which had me panting. We reluctantly pulled away, both reluctantly needing to breathe as I shot him a beaming smile which had him purring out in delight.

"Thanks" I beamed as I immediately got to work un-wrapping the straw and sticking it into my drink, the guys laughing as Hunter continued to purr behind me, obviously more than a little content with my reaction. We purred when we were content, happy or we used it as a way to comfort our mate when they were distressed: only shifters had the ability due to us having our wolf.

"You coming around tonight?" he asked hopefully when we had finished eating. It had been clear that he had been dying to ask since he had seen me and I couldn't help but shake my head amused as I took in the way his eyes seemed to sparkle with excitement.

"Sure" I smiled, it being the weekend tomorrow so I had nothing against either staying around his for the night or going home later than I usually did. The buses may have stopped so I couldn't get home that way but I could always run; it had after all been a while since I had been in my wolf form but I hadn't wanted anyone to spot me. That was not how I wanted Hunter to find out I could shift: while he was tracking me down to kill me for thinking I was a random rouge. Yep, didn't want that at all.

Chapter 26

Zoe's Pov

I was sitting propped up against a tree on the large fields surrounding the school, my mood switching between annoyance and understanding as I stared at the maths sums in front of me. Surprisingly my emotions had nothing to do with the fact the teacher had given all the students in his class a large amount of homework that even the smartest people would struggle with, it had nothing to do with the fact my pen had leaked over my work nor the fact I had left my sunglasses at home meaning I had no choice but to suffer through the annoying light as it glared off the pages in front of me. No, it had everything to do with the fact that I was stuck at school while my mate and the pack had to deal with a situation with a number of routes approaching their territory.

I knew that he was ok, of course he was and however cruel it may have sounded I wasn't worried about him. Not because I didn't care, I cared a lot for my mate, but I knew he was an amazingly werewolf and alpha and he would make sure nothing happened to him. I wasn't a clingy person by nature, I enjoy his company no end but I wasn't begging him to spend all his day with me. I wouldn't mind if I did don't get me wrong, but I didn't want to or feel the need to smother him or stalk him wherever he went like my pathetic sister.

The rouges had crossed the territory boarders and they had nothing to do with the school, meaning that by cutting across a packs territory it meant they were a threat that needed to be dealt with. Personally I had been attacked a number of times, I had always managed to get away of course since I was still breathing but that didn't mean I didn't have a few close times. I honestly thought it was disgusting how packs dealt with rouges, I like myself and a lot of other rogues here didn't become rouges by choice, we had no choice and yet we were hunted down because of it!

I scowled at my thoughts, wiping my black stained hands on the grass around me as I tried to clear away the ink which had leaked from my now useless pen. I was annoyed that they had left me even though I understood why; they didn't think I could shift so naturally I wouldn't have been much help if the situation would have turned serious. Never mind the fact that I was probably there best fighter, having the experience and such in attacking with the intent to kill.

Sighing I knew I couldn't blame him, but just sitting around doing nothing was a real pain in the arse. The fact I could be helping only making it worse, and I knew if anything happened to Hunter or my brother than I would never forgive myself. Even so I stayed put, not wishing for Hunter to find out that I could shift this way.

I wasn't going to keep it from him forever; actually I planned to tell him in the next few days if I built up enough courage to do so. I was worried about what his reaction would be, the fact not even my brother knew about my ability making the whole situation even worse. I knew he would flip out when he found out about it, probably demanding that I should have told him sooner. I found I wouldn't change it though, he may be my brother and I may love and trust him but the knowledge that I could shift kept my so-called parents from coming after me all those years.

When they had found out that Stacey could shift, she had been giving off the signs after all, they didn't let her out of their sights. Before a werewolf shifted, especially in a female on the rare occasion there were hints, tells that told the people around them what to expect. Such as the suddenly increased temperature, the mood swings and the fact that all of our senses grew stronger than a normal female werewolf. They had noticed hers of course when she was younger, but due to completely ignoring me I had to go through it all on my own without anyone.

I remembered that it was a both painful and terrifying experience, especially when you didn't know what was going on at the time. The feel of your bones breaking and realigning to support your new form for the first time was excruciatingly painful, the feeling while was necessary it was far from pleasing. It is the most painful thing a wolf will go through in their life, but the fact I was so young meant my pain tolerance as a child was even more sensitive, meaning the pain lasted for hours rather than the few minutes it was meant to.

Snapping out of my thoughts, not liking the depressing road they were going down I threw my books and notes to the side, not wanting to be bothered with them anymore. I wasn't an idiot by any means, but I also wasn't the smartest person, I had been a rogue all my life after all so school had never occurred to me. I had tried a human one once but it didn't turn out well, I found that while I may have looked like a human my inner wolf hated being surrounded by anyone other than its own kind. I only lasted about a few months before I couldn't take it anymore, choosing to spend my time in the woods or simply reading out of textbooks to teach myself.

Not wanting to dwell on the past since there was nothing I could do to change it I pulled my legs up to my chest, tilting my head back as I felt the bark of the tree press against me in a soothing manner. Being a werewolf meant our kind loved nature, loved woods and such since it was our wolves natural and instinctual surroundings. I just loved it for the sights, the smells and the sounds which were always surrounding you. The sound of the birds and the leaves, the smell of the different scents as they surrounded you and the fact everything looked to beautiful were all factors which appealed to me greatly.

I didn't know how long I sat there, the rest of the females sitting in class due to the bell not going yet. I had snuck out to sit outside, it was a gorgeous day out and I didn't see the need to waste it. It wasn't too hot but it was far from cold, the sun out making the grass shimmer attractively and a slight breeze in the air making it soothing to sit out.

It wasn't until all of the students started to filter out for lunch that I found myself watching them, my emerald eyes following their move-

ments as they talked and laughed as if the males of the pack weren't
off fighting. I may have had confidence in Hunter and Jack, but that
didn't mean I didn't worry about him. They were overconfident;
nothing good would come of it.

Hearing my phone go off I quickly slipped it out of my pocket, not
knowing who would be texting me right now since very few had my
number. Taking it out I frowned when I saw it was a number that I
didn't recognise, it stunning me slightly but I passed it off as someone
just having texted the wrong number. But as I looked at the text once
I opened it I felt my anger rise to an almost uncontrollable rate as I
read it, the words only fuelling my anger to a level which I knew I
wouldn't be able to control.

Last chance before no more Chloe it read causing my hands to
clench, my head snapping upright as I felt my wolf take over. It was
clearly from my parents, and as I looked to the right I felt my upper
lip pull back into a silent snarl as I noticed that a crowd had gathered.

My so called sister's scent filtered into my nose, the sharp and husky
aroma of it making it clear that she was in her wolf form. I was on my
feet instantly, my hands clenched so tightly that my knuckles turned
white with the strain when I took in what was in front of me. There
my bitch of a sister was, her large brown wolf viciously approaching
a terrified Chloe almost tauntingly, drawing out the fear. That was
the last thing I took in before I felt my wolf take over, the bond I had
with my brother meaning my wolf saw Chloe as a pack sister. The
fact she was under threat, under attack was unacceptable and my wolf
wanted to protect her family!

Chapter 27

H unters Pov
'Are you sure she's just not worried about you?' I asked
Jack through the pack mind as we headed back to the school, all of
us mated wolves eager to get back to our mates. Leaving them tended
to be painful, but I knew that the uncomfortable pull in my chest
would be nothing compared to what I would be like when I finally
mated and marked her as my own. When she was ready, which would
hopefully be soon, I would ravish her until she was screaming my
name as she withered underneath me before I sank my canines into
the flesh of her throat. The thought and mental image alone was
enough to have both me and my wolf panting, just knowing that in
the near future my fantasies would become my reality.

We had all been in our own thoughts when Jack suddenly picked
up his speed, mentioning something about getting a huge wave of
fear from Chloe and needing to get back to her since something was
wrong. I didn't question him, the rouges had been easily taken care

of and everyone was now breaking up to go their own ways. Since I had howled when I became aware of what was happening they had instantly dropped everything to come together as a group and fight, I didn't need to order them even though it was possible for me to do so. They were a loyal pack, each would fight to save their home and their loved ones – except for Stacy that was.

Ever since it had become common knowledge that we had a female shifter in the pack it had become both a blessing and a nightmare. The blessing being as simple as the fact it meant we could learn more about them, but then again that seemed to back fire since we couldn't be sure what she was telling us was the true or whether she was exaggerating to make herself sound better than she actually was. That wasn't the worst thing though, not only did she flaunt it around she made the other females of the pack feel like shit for not being born with the ability. To be honest it was pissing everyone off, it was only a matter of time before I had no choice but to put her in her place since some of the mated wolves were commenting on how she was upsetting their mates.

'This is something different, it's fear not worry he stated causing me to nod, telling everyone not to hold back and to get there as quickly as possible. Being the alpha I was naturally the fastest and strongest of the pack, but Collin wasn't far behind since he was my beta and Jack was surprisingly managing to keep up. I had a feeling that it was due to thinking his mate was in trouble, I knew that if I had had a similar feeling from Zoe then I would have been gone like a shot without looking back if it meant her safety was in danger.

It was with that thought I was suddenly filled with an anger which clearly wasn't my own, the feeling seemingly making my wolf see red as I was suddenly breaking off from the pack as my legs took me faster than the others could keep up with. I didn't know what was happening, but something was making my mate boil with such anger that I didn't realise she was capable of. Something was definitely wrong. My mate while she had her own problems was a down to earth girl and I loved that about her; but the rage I was feeling off her was so strong that she shouldn't have been able to feel something so powerful, so raw.

'What's wrong?' Collin asked through the mind link causing me growl slightly, not at my beta of course but at the realisation that something could be wrong with her. My mate was too delicate, too valuable to me for anything to be a threat to her! She was mine!

'Something's not right' I stated as I continued to push myself harder along with Jack, who hearing my thoughts and worry on Zoe only seemed to try and push himself harder due to the fact that both his sister and mate could be in trouble. I didn't blame him; hell I was already quite a large distance from the pack before I heard Collins thoughts in my head as he tried to keep up with me along with the others.

'Hunter you need to try and calm down, if something is wrong then wouldn't it be safer to have the us with you?' he asked me gently, making sure not to make his voice a demand which would only infuriate my wolf more than he already was as he would have felt as if a pack mate was stepping out of line. I felt Collin shudder at my thoughts, making me realise that I had kept my mind open for all to hear as I did so.

'He has a point mate, let us help' Josh stated as well, though his own thoughts were on Hannah as he worried about her as well. I didn't blame him, but he had stated with the others that while her emotions were a little haywire she didn't seem to be in any immediate danger which he was thankful for.

I couldn't help but feel jealous with how easily they could feel their mates, all of my close pack mates having already claimed their mates for all to see. I knew they had taken into consideration of how much it was taking out of me to hold back my wolf who wanted nothing more than to mount my mate at every opportunity he had to do so, the pack making sure not to make any comments around her which would risk triggering my possessiveness which would only make it harder for me to control my inner beast. He wanted to protect his mate of course, but he thought that the only way to do so was to mark her so he could keep track of her and make sure she was safe. I knew she wasn't ready for it so I held back for her sake, I would never force myself on her!

It worked like that for every mated couple, though alphas felt it stronger. I knew that as soon as I sank my canines into that slender neck of hers that I would be filled with both my emotions and hers, feeling them in such detail that I would always know what mood she was in. It was designed for me to make sure that she was always safe and happy around me; though I had no idea what it would be like if the female could shift as well since it would affect her inner wolf as well as the males. See this was the problem, how little we knew of female shifters and while we had hoped Stacy would fill us in we couldn't trust a word that came out of her mouth and the whole pack knew it.

'It won't be too long until she'll cave mate, we all see how she looks at you' Liam stated before my head was filled with his memoires, showing me using the pack mind of the times he had watched us. I couldn't help but give a wolfy grin when I saw the adoration which was present in her eyes as she looked at me, how much she seemed to be in tuned to me as he showed me a picture of her curled up on my lap as we all watched a film at the pack house. It was kind of shocking when she had told us all that she enjoyed watching horrors over romances, mentioning how she couldn't never grasp on why you would want to watch a film that left you in tears. Did I mention how incredible my mate was?

'Yea Hunter, just image she'll be under you soon enough' Josh smirked causing my mind to immediately be drawn to just that. Mm, I couldn't wait until she finally caved. I knew I was starting to have an effect on her, letting my touches linger a little more than necessary, letting my arm brush against the swell of those tempting breasts of hers....

'Dude I know you're the alpha and she's your mate and all, but that's my fucking sister!' Jacks thoughts slammed into my brain causing the tension to break as I could hear the mental laughter of the pack as they couldn't help but release wolfy chuckles that sounded far from normal in their animal forms. I couldn't help but roll my eyes,

Zoe was my mate god-dammit so I should be able to think about her when I wanted! But unfortunately I could kind of see where he was coming from; for his sake I will try and tone it down.

'Thanks mate' his thoughts hit me again causing me to roll my eyes at how relieved he sounded.

'I'm not making any promises' I stated in my head as we continued to head to the school, my mates emotions still worrying me but it was nice to have a distraction so I didn't completely loose it. I could tell that Jack was pleased as well, both of us thinking that Stacy was still there so if something was wrong she would be able to let us know via the pack mind. I could sense that she was phased; hopefully she was guarding the woods like I told her to.

She had wanted to come of course but I had denied it much to the relief of the pack, she was fast yes but she was to put it bluntly stupid when it came to instincts. She ignored them basically. When her wolf told her to flee she stood her ground and when her wolf told her to fight she either froze or then decided to run when we actually needed her help. It was because of this that she was a reliability and it was better that she just stayed away, it was too risky having her close to the fight since we would always have to be looking out for her which mean we were less concentrated on the battle. So with that I ordered her to stay around the school, an order which she couldn't refuse even if she tried to. It was built into your wolf to want to obey an order from an alpha; a wolf lived for three things; to mate, to protect your home and to obey an alpha.

'Still, thanks' he replied with relief making me roll my eyes at his tone, I could only picture what it would look like on my wolf form but I couldn't be sure.

'How's the whole mating thing coming along?' Liam asked curiously, his thoughts on Kelly as the rest of my pack seemed to be just as curious to what my answer would be. They wanted an alpha female along with their wolves, the fact I had been running the pack solo for years without a mate at my side practically unheard of. A mate was meant to be there to keep the alpha level headed, to help look after the pack and such and the fact I didn't officially have one since I had yet to claim her meant every pack mates wolves were restless.

'God it's getting harder and harder to hold back mate, seriously she walks around in my clothes for goodness sakes!' I almost whimpered out as I remembered how she would walk around the pack house in my shirt and boxers, mentioning how she liked the fact that they were smothered in my scent and she liked the way the fabric felt as it touched her skin. I mean did she know how much it was taking out of me not to rip the bloody things off her and pound her into the bed sheets? I mean she looked so fucking edible that I could barely keep my hands off her when she was around, refusing to leave her alone when she was walking about since my wolf wouldn't allow it due to his possessive side. He didn't like his mate walking around while looking so delicious since she wasn't marked yet. I vaguely wondered if she had noticed, how I had always made an excuse to follow her around even though I had tried to be subtle about it.

'I think we've all noticed that alpha, she isn't exactly making it easy on you' Josh sniggered, thinking back to when he met Hannah. The chemistry between them had been instant, but she had teased and taunted him for weeks before finally giving in with a grin. It had been hilarious to watch, but that didn't mean I found it funny when I was on the receiving end even though I knew Zoe wasn't doing it on purpose.

'I know, she's worth it' and she was, she was so worth it. She was worth the pull in my chest when she was away from me, the way my wolf snarled that she wasn't mated and marked and the fact he was constantly restless for not having his alpha-female by his side constantly where she belonged. But she was worth waiting for, the gorgeous girl who had been through so much in her short life meant enough to me to make me fight my urges.

'You know Hunter, while I hate to have to see the mental images which flash through my head when you picture what you think she might look like naked, I'm glad you're the one she's going to mate with' Jack stated quietly in his head causing me to both blush slightly in my wolf form and grin, thankful that no one could see me go bright red while I was my wolf.

Since I was the alpha it meant that I could easily hide my thoughts from others, but I tended to forget and the rest of the pack got a...eyeful to say the least. It wasn't like I had seen her naked unfortunately so neither me or my wolf minded, when it came to making love to your mate the males tended to be able to keep it out of the thoughts of the others. It seemed natural, for the wolf in you to feel possessive enough not to want others to see what your mate looked like naked. Not that anyone was complaining, our wolves were possessive enough as it is without knowing that others had seen so much of your lover, your soul-mate.

'Thanks Jack, it means a lot' I said sincerely, a compliment from your alpha meaning a lot to both the pack mate and their wolf. I knew this which was why I rarely thanked someone so sincerely, not because I was ungrateful but because I knew how much it meant to a person's wolf to be accepted and thanked by an alpha of your pack.

'No problem Hunter, any time' was his grinning reply before everyone had managed to catch up with me, making me realise that I had been further ahead of them then I realised. I had slowed down to a jog when I found it made sense to wait for them, safety and power in numbers after all. It would have been entirely different if I had felt fear from Zoe instead of just anger; however cruel it may have sounded if my mate was in trouble then she was my first priority, even over my pack.

'So what's the plan-' Collin stated as we reached the school only for each of us to freeze as we took in the scene in front of us, Collins voice zoning off as we all found ourselves frozen in place. I didn't know what I had been expecting, but it was definitely not this.

Chapter 28

Hunters Pov

I didn't know why but I found it impossible to move as I took in the scene in front of me, a quick glance to my pack mates only causing me to realise that they were in the exact same situation. Due to my inner wolf being the alpha he effectively 'owned' you could call it each and every wolf that lived inside my pack, it was what made it possible for me to command them. But as I took in the scene in front of me, frozen to the spot, I couldn't help but take in the fact that they stood stiff and unwillingly as if I had given them an alpha command even though I hadn't.

My wolf was telling me that I needed to watch this, that it would ruin everything if I intervened however much I wanted to. My mate was practically committing suicide in front of me but however much I struggled with my wolf I couldn't move, I hated it! I hated the fact I felt weak against my own animal, to wound up with worry and panic to realise just how necessary it was for me to pay attention and watch.

How both mine and the packs future was about to chance right in front of our eyes, how much more possessive my inner wolf was going to act until my mate was fully claimed like I had craved since I had first found out that she was mine; that she was my soul-mate and my other half.

'What the fuck is going on?' Jack asked panicked as he found it impossible to move much like myself, the alpha wolf in me taking complete charge of the pack. I knew he was acting by instinct, but with my mate in danger as well as Jacks I couldn't help but want to ignore it. I could already begin to feel myself resenting my inner alpha, not knowing that in mere minutes I would be kissing the ground he walked on.

'I don't know!' went around the pack mind as we all took in the scene in front of us, terrified out of our minds and helpless to act against what we thought was inevitable.

I watched as I took in what was happening in front of me, how Stacy's large brown wolf was standing threateningly in front of a terrified Chloe as she tried to back away only to find her back pressing against the back of a tree preventing her from moving any further. What the hell was Stacy playing at? Was she seriously planning to attack one of our own? One of our mated females? Was she stupid?

"Stacy please, I don't know what I've wrong" we were all forced to listen to Chloe beg, Jack not even being able to snarl as it seemed as if our inner wolves were refusing to make ourselves known. I didn't know why, but I knew something big was going to happen as I tried to fight my wolf only to find it pointless in doing so. My wolf had full control, and to be honest it was scaring the shit out of me.

Stacy's wolfy chuckles filtered into our ears as each and every one of us felt the fur on our backs raise as we watched the only female wolf of the pack taunt Jacks mate. It was clear Chloe was terrified out of her mind, we could practically smell the fear as it came off her in waves as Stacy continued to play with her as if she meant nothing, as if she was food in the wild! It was disgusting and as soon as I got my wolf under control she was going to pay!

It was when I felt my gaze drawn to my right that I felt my eyes widen and my panic increase, catching sight of my mate as she seemed to be watching the scene in front of her with pure anger in her gaze. Oh please don't do anything stupid baby I begged in my mind, whimpering slightly as I doubled my efforts to move only to find it pointless as none of us could move from our positions from the edge of the woods. What the hell was going on?

It was then I felt the previous anger I felt from my mate radiate through my body at such a level that I found it affecting my own, only increasing my own anger and frustration as I felt my ears twitch on the top of my head before pulling back in a threatening manner as I felt my upper lip rise in a silent snarl. What on earth was my wolf playing at?

"Oh fuck no" I heard my mate hiss as I watched helplessly as she stumbled to her feet, the venom in her tone causing even me to flinch as I noticed my pack mates do the same. It was clear the others were thankful their mates were not involved and were safe, even if they trembled with the others as they watched the scene in front of them with fear in their eyes.

'Holy shit Hunter, what the fuck is she doing?' Josh exclaimed as we all watched wide eyed and speechless as my mate suddenly started to sprint in the direction of where Stacy was still taunting Chloe, my eyes watching her helplessly as I felt myself whining at how much danger she was putting herself into. She didn't stand a chance against Stacy; she was a female not a shifter! What was she doing, didn't she care that she was putting herself in danger!

'No baby, please no' I found myself whining over and over again as I tried to fight against my wolf only to come up short, why was my wolf letting her do this? Here in front of us our mate was clearly going to get hurt and yet all I could hear him whispering to me is that she would be fine, that I needed to see something. I hated it, loathed it even as I felt my anger rise at both Stacy and my wolf. I wanted answers, and I wanted them now!

It wasn't until she got half way and started to take off her shirt that I felt my previous struggling halt instantly, my head tilting to the side as her suddenly lime coloured green bra came into view. If I hadn't of been so distracted with my mates' actions I probably would have chuckled at her choice of colour for her bra, or glazed lustfully at her generous chest as her breasts bounced deliciously with even step she took. But I was distracted, distracted with the fact that she now running at a speed not even a female should have been capable of.

None of us could even think to each other as we watched her shirt hit the ground before blowing slightly in the wind, her shoes next to go before she somehow managed to get her skirt off while running revealing a sight that had my wolf moaning and purring in delight. Her legs looked so fucking long, her stomach toned and flat clueing me in on the fact she exercised a lot and her chest....just uh!

It wasn't that what had my attention though surprisingly, my form to shocked to even think of trying to move again as I watched the air rippled around her just as she reached Stacy's still distracted wolf. What happened next I couldn't believe my eyes, Zoe phasing so quickly before suddenly the most gorgeous white wolf suddenly appeared in her place as she phased mid step, something which I thought was impossible.

I couldn't help but take in her wolf, the size of it slightly bigger than Stacy's but still smaller than my more than impressive size. I was the alpha after all. A few black markings were on her snowy white fur, her paw and ear pitch black making her look anything other than deadly, that was until she pulled the upper lip of her muzzle up revealing a set of perfectly white canines which seemed to be out for blood.

My Zoe, my mate was a shifter! My mate was a shifter!

I watched with keen eyes as the claws of her paws on her front legs dug into the soft ground before she kicked off with her hind legs to gain leverage, all of this happening so quickly, so effortlessly that everyone watching could only gaze on in pure shock and amazement as my mate pounced onto Stacy's still unaware form catching her by surprise.

Her howl of shock and agony filtered into our sensitive ears but none of us cared, Chloe screaming out in surprise as the large brown wolf was suddenly knocked over before my mates glistening teeth sank into her sister's neck with no remorse. I still couldn't help but be scared for her though, Stacy had been trained whilst my mate hadn't of been. It was unnecessary though since as soon as her teeth had made contact with Stacy's brown fur it was obvious to us all that Stacy didn't stand a chance in hell of winning.

Chloe had instantly run towards the females of the pack who were close to my mate once Stacy's large wolf was taken down without hesitation, everyone's eyes on the two large wolves as Zoe effortlessly threw Stacy to the floor causing another howl of pain to fall from her lips. Again none of us cared, only being able to watch on as my mate got into a defensive pose in front of all of the pack females much to the relief of my pack mates. The fact she was protecting our soul-mates, our other half's like a mother would her cubs meant that each and every one of them saw her as the alpha-female that she was born to be.

We continued to watch as Stacy hurriedly got back onto her feet; my mates muzzle now dark with blood that clearly wasn't her own; the wound on Stacy's neck only making it more obvious whose blood it actually was. Stacy's snarl rang through the woods as she got into an attacking pose, my wolf not liking the fact she was being aggressive to my mate but keeping the command in place knowing that I needed to see this, to see my mate as my complete and utter equal, as my alpha-female, as my other-half!

The two circled each other, all of us not believing our eyes as we watched how foolish Stacy was being. It wasn't like I was cheering her on, hell no, but the fact she was denying the clearly instinctual urge to submit to the female alpha meant that it was suicide, she didn't stand a chance but that didn't mean I worried any less for my mates safety like any male wouldn't.

Stacy tried to take my mate by surprise, but anyone could see that Zoe was prepared for it. I mean even the females of the pack cringed slightly when Stacy made her move out of reflex, knowing what a foolish decision it was going to be on her part. So as soon as Stacy leapt for my mate she soon found my Zoe's teeth firmly imbedded in her neck, all of us cringing as our sensitive hearing picked up the crunching sound as Zoe held nothing back as she attacked her own sister as if she was a stranger. I guess she was if I thought about it, making sure to block my thoughts from the pack as I realised that all Zoe had been through the only family she actually considered to be one was Jack.

With that thought I knew she wouldn't care if she killed Stacy, and by the way everyone was backing away as she threw Stacy's now limp wolf around as if she was nothing it was clear that was exactly what she was going to do if I didn't stop her.

Feeling my wolf release the command after my realisation, my wolf now purring at the thought of my mate being a shifter as I sprinted quickly across the field towards my mate who picked up on the movement instantly. Good girl I thought with pride, such a talented and protective wolf.

Letting go of Stacy's neck her body hit the ground with a thump, the pack doctor standing nervously at the side along with the school staff as everyone was still in shock over what they had just discovered. My mate had hid her wolf so easily, so efficiently that I couldn't help but be both annoyed and impressed as I trotted over to her to make sure she didn't see me as a threat. She didn't thankfully, my form stopping just in front of hers as my large black wolf contrasted amazingly against hers as I bend my head down slightly to bump my muzzle against her bloody one.

I whined slightly when she backed away from me, her large emerald eyes wide with what looked like fear as she stumbled back on her legs. It was a sharp contrast to what her previous gracefully and calculated moves had been when she had taken down Stacy with such viciousness that I couldn't help but find it arousing.

'We have to get her away from Stacy mate, I may hate the girl but do you really want to deal with the consequences of her death right now?' Collins voice filtered into my head, the others having phased but Collin as my beta had resisted the urge to appear near his mates side to do his job. It was why I choose him as beta, a decision I would never regret.

'Aw thanks mate, I'm touched' his thoughts hit me causing me to shake my head at his amused tone, but he was right I didn't want to deal with the consequences which would come if Stacy died. Turning back to my angel I took note that she had relaxed, her large wolf head tilted to the left as she seemed to be studying me in detail. Unfortunately I wouldn't be able to hear her in my head until I had mated with her, again hopefully I wouldn't have to wait long.

Barking at her I approached her playfully, wagging my tail to show how happy I am that she could phase even if I was hurt that she had kept it from me. I could understand why of course, hell not even her brother knew since if he did he would have told me when I had alpha ordered what seemed like ages ago. Hopefully she would trust me to tell me about herself, my hopes only increasing now we had a female shifter that I could trust! I knew my mate was amazing, but this was just incredible!

Chapter 29

Hunters Pov

I didn't know what was going through that head of hers but the last thing I expected her to do was run from me, the white behind of her wolf flashing through the woods before she was gone like a shot. To be honest it hurt, a lot, that she was running away from me but I knew she must be feeling a number of conflicting emotions right now. She had just exposed her clearly deeply personal secret of being a wolf, one she had kept hidden from everyone who knew her for her whole life, to protect a female of her pack. And it was her pack as well as mine, it was our pack and as soon as she let me claim her we would run it together like we were destined to.

'I've got this alpha, go after her!' Collin stated, clearing seeing how conflicted I felt. It was my duty as alpha to check if Stacy was ok, I may hate her but she was still a pack member. Zoe on the other hand was my life, my other half; my mate and I wanted nothing more than to run after her since I could almost feel the pain she was going through. So when Collin stated he would take over the situation I was off like a shot, my claws gripping the soft ground with every pounce as I headed as quickly as I could through the woods, running after my angel as if my life depending on it.

'Thanks mate, I owe you one' I thought back to Collin as I followed my mates scent, the fact she had now shifted in front of us all meant that it would be impossible to hide her scent. I knew what it smelt like now, and while it was shocking that she had managed to hide it for so long now it was out in the open she would be a lot easier to find.

'Don't worry about it' was all I got back before I shut the mind link between us, my nose lowering to the ground as I breathed in deeply as I followed her scent to where she had gone.

It didn't take long until I found her, her light pants filling the air as she seemed to be sniffing a large clearing as she trotted around it almost causally. I could see how at unease she was though, her form stiff and her ears twitched back as her bloody face and muzzle continued to scan the area as she paced, clearly not knowing what to do with herself now she had ran.

Whimpering lowly in my throat her head snapped in my direction, the fact she knew instantly where to look cluing me in on the fact she knew I was following the whole time. It didn't surprise me, my mate was both incredibly smart and special.

Don't run baby....please I mentally pleaded with her when I saw her claws dig into the ground hinting me in on the fact that she was preparing to run. I couldn't help but whine louder, lowering my large form to the ground to try and show her that I wasn't a threat. She must know that I could and would never hurt her, but if I had to show submission to my mate then I would do so without regret.

I could tell the action surprised her, her form relaxing slightly due to how stunned she seemed. I knew why she was, I mean it went against all of my nature to not submit and yet here I was on the ground in front of my mate. I hoped beyond hope that it would show her how much I cared; how much I trusted and loved her and when I saw her slowly start to approach me I knew I had thankfully succeeded.

Slowly getting up I lowered my head to hers when she stood in front of me, her white wolf while larger than most still looked tiny compared to mine as I bumped my muzzle gently against hers in a soft and loving manner. I couldn't help but let my tail sway side to side quickly when I felt her return the gesture, the previous gap between us closing as I felt her rub her nose into the pelt of my neck as she nuzzled against me causing me to purr.

I couldn't help but return the gesture, my heavy tongue lolling out of the side of my mouth as I ran it over her healthy white fur over and over again as if we were true wolves in the wild. I was comforting my mate, and as I felt and heard her purr in her own chest I couldn't help but press myself against her, my wolf howling in pure pleasure as I walked around her as I took her all in.

I made sure to always keep contact as I brushed around her, not being able to resist however much I tried to not to breathe in the musky scent of her rear as her tail raised automatically at my action. A low but animistic growl rippled from my throat as I found my wolf going nuts with the sudden urge to claim her, he wanted nothing more than to mount her right there and then but the last thing I wanted was for our first time to be in wolf form. I wanted to feel her soft skin as she moved against me, feel her lips on mine as I took her to heights of pleasure which she wouldn't have thought possible. So with that on my mind I held back the wolf in me before returning to her front, her face moving to press against my neck as we both felt a slight breeze from when our tails were wagging happily.

I didn't know how long we stood there until I saw and heard her thump her bottom end on the floor, her tongue lolling out of the side of her mouth as she looked up at me with those gorgeous amber eyes of hers. Amber was the colour of all of our wolves' eyes once we had phased, but the shades were different and unique for each and every shifter. Zoe's eyes were as vibrant as they come; the colour standing out against her light coat making her look even more beautiful to me if that was possible.

Joining her on the ground I let myself sit beside her, my head resting on the back of her neck as we continued to sit in silence, enjoying each other's company before I felt the familiar feeling in my head meaning someone wanted to talk to me.

'How are things alpha?' I heard Collin ask as soon as I had opened my mind to him, letting him see through my eyes how my mate was wrapped around me as I rested my head on her back. I could sense his awe, not only at the fact she was a female wolf but the fact she had managed to hide it from us for so long. I made a mental note to ask her about how she managed to mask her scent, it was incredibly impressive and much like watching her when she phased mid-stride I thought it had been impossible until I had seen my angel do it right in front of my eyes.

'Good, how are Stacy, Jack and Chloe?' I asked with a slight wince, not knowing whether I wanted Stacy to be alright or not. She deserved everything she got and once I got back then she was going to be punished, there was no way I wanted such a spoilt brat in my pack and the sooner her and her pathetic parents were gone the better. She had pushed and pushed but now she had gone way to far, you do NOT threaten someone's mate, especially a female like she had been doing. It was sick, barbaric and incredibly frowned upon and if she thought what my mate did to her was the end of it then she was so very wrong.

'Jacks pissed as you can imagine but thankfully she's alright and safe, Chloe's worried about your mate even though I told her Zoe was fine and Stacy...well let's just say it will take her weeks to heal at least, I didn't know how Zoe managed to do it but she managed to shatter every bone in Stacy's body without puncturing any of her internal organs' he stated with awe in his tone, clearly impressed that even though it looked like my mate was killing Stacy all she had done was inflict masses of pain on her. Again I couldn't help but release a wolfy grin; my mate was awesome!

'Is the pack doctor looking at her?' I asked, wanting to know what was going on with my pack. I really needed to be there but as I felt my mates wet muzzle burry itself against my coat I knew that I had to stay, not that I was complaining since the feel of my mate next to me in wolf form was incredibly satisfying. I think it was down to the fact that my wolf had never been so content, not to mention I would get to spend all of my day with her now since she would have to be transferred to the classes which involved the males because of the shifting. While I didn't like so many unmated males around her when I had yet to claim her I knew they wouldn't even try and get too close to her, just the thought of them touching her made me want to rip out there throats and I was only imagining it!

'Yep she's on bed rest...' he trailed off uncomfortably, clearing knowing something that I didn't. I couldn't help but feel my wolf start to get restless, the thought that a pack mate was keeping something from me, friend or not, was completely unacceptable.

'Spill!' I ordered, letting a little of my alpha order slip through just enough for him to feel it. I could tell he did, sensing his shiver as he didn't even try and fight my control over him as he instantly came clean with a wince.

'There's another problem, it's her parents-' he started causing me to naturally growl, Zoe jumping slightly before I let a comforting purr rumble in my chest before she relaxed against me again causing me to grin. That's a good girl.

'What about the bastards?' I mentally snarled causing him to flinch, I didn't care. Just the thought of that family made my wolf turn red with rage, only Jack and Zoe mattered to me from that family the rest could die in hell for all I cared. Call me harsh but I don't care, they kicked my mate out when she was a child and there other daughter just tried to harm a mated female. Both were unacceptable in my books and they would be dealt with!

'They are demanding to stay at the pack house while Stacy recovers-' he started but I cut him off with another vicious growl which I knew they could all hear from the school grounds, his flinch of both fear and un-comfort told me that.

'There is no way in hell that is happening!' I snarled through the pack mind, I did not want those people in my house! Stacy was going as soon as she recovered enough so I didn't want them there, not to mention I knew my mate wouldn't stay at my home if they were present and that was just not happening. I was going to ask her to move in but I knew she would out right deny it if I let them stay, so nope, they were out of there!

'I agree with you alpha. Jack is flipping out but Chloe is managing to keep him calm enough not to shift, but that's not the worst bit' he stated with agreement, I knew he would back me up the entire way if I kicked them out. Actually I could hear his thoughts, he wanted me to and was actually hoping to sway my decision. Not that I minded, my decision was already made up and the last thing I wanted was for them to stay at the place I called my home.

'What could be worse than that?' I asked, not knowing what he thought would upset me more than the bastards wanting to not only move into my house but to stay there for weeks. I mean I knew that their house burnt down but it was getting re-built; they stopped being classed as a pack member of mine as soon as I heard what they did to my mate, to a child less than the age of a teen! They mean nothing to me!

'You're not going to like it, at all' he thought quietly, but I could sense how reluctant he was to tell me since his own disgust and anger over that whatever it was came through loud and clear. What could be bad enough to upset my beta in such a way?

'Tell me!' at this point I didn't bother to hold back any of my alpha order, feeling his own wolf cave instantly making it impossible for him to hold anything back for me even if he wanted to. If something had happened to cause my normally relaxed and in control beta to feel such anger over a situation then it must have been bad, I wanted, no needed to know what the hell was behind it!

'They want Zoe punished, saying that she attacked their daughter without a good enough reason' he quickly got out, my furious roar filling the forest as I felt everyone in my pack shun back in pure fear at the sound of it. My wolf was furious, my previous sitting and relaxing form now pacing and circling my mate in a protective manner which was instinctual. How dare they think they have the right, the fucking nerve to tell me I had to punish me mate! I would kill them all before I even thought of doing such a thing!

I was brought out of my anger filled haze when I heard my mate whimper slightly, snapping out of it only to do the same when I caught sight of her shunned back form as she curled herself in as I circled her. I knew it wasn't out of fear, I could feel that my mate didn't fear me which I was so fucking thankful for. No, I could tell that she wanted nothing more than to come and comfort me but was trying to give me the impression of space.

Not wanting her to feel any doubt that I wanted her near me I quickly totted over to her, pressing myself against her as I repeating licked her coat in a comforting and caring manner, feeling her do the same to me as I did so. She was my life; I would kill anything that brought any harm to her. She was it for me now, I would be a shell of a wolf if I didn't have her with me and I refused to put her in any risk.

'Where are they?' I asked more calmly, my mates calming touch and presence helping me push back my anger as I concentrated on my angel as she pressed herself firmly against me, her wet and heavy tongue lapping at my ear causing my back leg to twitch in pleasure. Uh....god that felt so good...

'Who Stacy's parents?' he asked causing me to mentally sigh; who else would I be talking about?

'Yea' I replied, howling slightly in pleasure as I felt Zoe increase the pressure on my ear as I lowered my head so she could have more room to work with. Fuck, it felt like pure heaven.

'Currently their at the pack house, why?' he asked, clearly wanting nothing more than for me to go over and sort them the hell out. Well he wasn't about to be disappointed.

'We're on our way' I stated before I shut the link, trotting over to Zoe's rear end as I gently nudged her back in the direction of the school, trying to ignore how feminine and musky she smelt in her wolf form. It was making my wolf go ballistic with the want to claim her, the want to sink his canines into her throat as a warning sign that she was taken, that I would hunt down and kill all whoever harmed her in any way. She is mine, and I would protect her until my last breath...

Chapter 30

Hunters Pov

Running beside my mate was thrilling to say the least, her side brushing against mine as I made sure to keep her in sight at all times. I hadn't yet spoken to her out of wolf form so I had no idea what was going through that pretty head of hers, hell it could be anything and even though I hated to admit it I was worried she would run off again.

Shaking my head I couldn't help but nuzzle my nose in the pelt of her fur, my muzzle pressing against her neck as we continued to run. She smelt so good to my wolf, her musky female essence making it even harder to fight back on the urge to claim her like both me and my wolf wanted to. I wouldn't push her though; I loved her too much for that.

It was with that thought I nearly lost my footing, did I love her? I knew as soon as I tried to deny it that it was true, she meant everything to me and I knew that even if our kind didn't have mates I would have still fallen for her sooner or later. She was everything in a girl that I wanted, she was sweet, funny, sexy of course but she also protective, smart and honest. All traits which should be present in an alpha female and I couldn't have been more thankful that the spirits had destined her to belong to me as I did her.

Heading in the direction of the pack house I turned a sharp right only for Zoe to slowly slow from the run we had been in to a trot, making me frown before quickly dashing back to her side. It was times like these the fact our minds weren't connected was a real pain, but again I wasn't going to force her to mate with me if she wasn't ready, I would wait even if it would take a lot of control to hold back my wolf since he was more than ready to be bound to her for eternity.

I let a whine escape my muzzle as I trotted towards her, trying to portray my confusion over what she was up to. She seemed to think it over for a few moments before she took off in the opposite direction, my worst fears becoming a reality as I shot after her as quick as a bullet. Why was she running away from me? She seemed fine before, so what had changed?

My wolf howled and snarled in protest though, not taking note that the direction she was going was actually to the school and that she wasn't just running off somewhere in the woods. No I didn't realise this until my claws had dug into the soft grass underneath me, my hind legs pushing me off the ground as I pounced on my escaping mate with such power that it caused us both to tumble to the ground harshly.

Her high pitched whine quickly had me springing to action though, removing my large body from hers as soon as possible when I took note of the awkward angle she was lying under me in. Oh shit....

Shifting back into human form, the fact I was naked for all to see not bothering me as I quickly moved towards my mate with a pained and regretful expression. I hadn't meant to be so rough with her, but the thought that she was running from me had caused my wolf to momentarily take control as he followed his instincts to calm his wolf. It was due to us not being mated, since in the animal world she would still be considered up for grabs which was why my wolf was so possessive of her. He didn't want to lose her, and neither did I.

"Shit, are you already baby?" I asked with worry when she hadn't moved for a while, seemingly stunned before she jumped to her feet while shaking out her fur. She seemed to look at me curiously; her head tilted to the side before she used her nose to bump my ankle, trying to avoid looking at the junction between my legs were my member laid. I couldn't help but smirk, such an innocent little girl I thought with a grin.

"Oh shit, you were going to get your clothes?" I asked guiltily when I realised she was gesturing to the outfit I had tied to my right leg, feeling bad for tackling her when I thought she was trying to run from me. She must have been running back to the academy to get her clothes, though I had a feeling that one of the pack members may have already taken them back to the pack house so the journey would have been pointless.

Hearing her bark in agreement I quickly bent down to unstrap the thin shirt I had attached to my leg, not wanting to let her out of my sights while the threat of her parents wanting to punish her was still out in the open. Just the thought that they had the nerve to even think that I would ever do such a thing was vile, a male would never punish their mate, ever! So the simple realisation that they thought I was going to was purely naïve and stupid of them, bloody bastards!

"Here" I gestured as I held out my shirt for her, it would be long enough to cover all of her goods, unfortunately. But then again it would help with the whole not claiming her yet, I could only hope that she would be ready soon since I didn't know how much longer I could hold my wolf back from getting what he wanted. Alpha wolves were stronger after all, I was born to lead and I was born to do it with a mate by my side. That mate was Zoe.

I watched as she seemed to hesitate for a moment, her gaze glancing from the shirt in my hand before moving to my eyes. After what seemed like only minutes she gently took the clothing I was offering her into her mouth before dashing into the forest, my hearing picking up on how she only went a few feet as to change in private. I didn't know whether to be disappointed or relieved that she was making it easier for me to resist pouncing and mounting her right there and then.

It was when she came out of the forest and into the clearing where I stood half-dressed that I felt my breath catch in my throat, having slipped on a pair of shorts when she was gone as not to make her uncomfortable. I had nothing wrong against being in the nude since

I was more than adequate size wise even for a werewolf, but I didn't want to scare her off if she thought I was expecting something more from her than her love and company. Sex could wait as far as I was concerned.

Saying that though I couldn't help but take in the sight in front of me, my mate, my very sexy and nervous looking mate shifting from foot to foot wearing nothing other than my shirt. It glided off her curves in a manner which made me want to purr, she looked so good...

"Hunter!" she snapped amused gaining my attention, a sheepish smile forming on my lips as she rolled her eyes but approached me anyway. She still seemed nervous I found, as if she thought I would be angry or disappointed that she had hidden something so life-changing from me. I couldn't find it in me to be angry with her though, she was my mate not to mention I was too happy to even think of telling her off about it.

"I'm not angry baby" I smiled as I pulled her into my arms, trying to ignore how delectable she felt against me as I wrapped my arms around her waist. I couldn't resist pulling her flush against me, my nose buried in her neck as I breathed in that all to delicious scent of hers. How did she always seem to smell so good to me? It was addicting!

"Why?" she asked quietly, as if she couldn't understand my reaction to learning about her precious secret.

"What you did Zoe was courageous of you, you revealed your well-kept secret to us to protect the pack and for that reason I can be anything but angry with you" I murmured honestly, pressing my lips to the flesh of her neck. I stayed clear of where I wanted to mark her though, not knowing if I would be able to control my wolf and the last thing I wanted was a momentarily lapse in judgement.

"Thank you" she said so softly that I wasn't sure whether she meant for me to hear it or not. Even so I did and it filled me with so much warmth that I couldn't help but tilt her head up my hand and press my lips gently to hers, relishing in everything about my mate from her taste to her smell. She was perfect, so perfect.

"You have nothing to be thankful for baby, I should be the one thanking you" I mumbled against her lips, growling slightly in plea-sure when I felt her arms wrap around my neck in an intimate gesture which had both of us panting. I loved how responsive to my touch she was, how much I affected her as she affected me. She was mine, she was made for me and I would never be letting her go.

"You have no idea how lucky I feel Hunter, no idea at all" I heard her whisper to herself, even with my sensitive hearing I found it difficult to pick it up leading me to the conclusion that the last thing she had expected was for me to hear it. I couldn't help but grin though, deepening the kiss after pulling her lips back to mine as I let my own tongue explore her mouth in a gentle and loving manner.

It was when I heard her moan against me, pressing her breasts against my bare chest that she soon found her back pressed rough-ly up against the bark of a tree. Our kisses grew deeper and more frenzied, our breathing sharper and more uneven as we only pulled away to breath before crashing our lips together in another passionate embrace.

We were snapped out of it when a howl could be heard from the pack house, a sigh falling from my bruised and swollen lips as I recognised it as Collin's. I suppose he had expected us back a lot sooner, but it was hardly my fault that we got distracted and started making out heavily against a tree. Even though it wasn't what I expected for our first time I wouldn't have complained, hell no but I knew that she deserved better than that.

With that thought I reluctantly pulled away, her legs somehow having wrapped themselves around my waist and with the sudden knowledge of how close our sexes were I knew we had to find another position before I couldn't control myself.

"Come on" I smiled, loving it when she whimpered when I pulled away. I couldn't help but shake my head amused, though the smirk on her own swollen lips had me groaning as she grinded herself against me in a teasing manner which had my back arching and a animalistic growl falling from my lips. God, what was she doing to me?

"Cock blocker" I swore I heard her mutter as she jumped from my arms, her bare feet touching the ground with a slight thud as I felt my jaw go slack with her comment. Did she seriously just say that? But the look of smugness and amusement on her face told me that I had in fact heard her correctly, my little mate just had the cheek to call me a cock-blocker.

"Oh, I'll show you cock-blocker" I growled playfully causing her to giggle, the sound making me smile despite myself as she spun around me in a childish manner which had my wolf purring at the sight of joy on her face. I was again reminded of my previous thoughts on her; she really was a free spirit.

"So why are we in a rush back?" she asked curiously as she continued to dance around me, my eyes trained on her bare legs as she moved on the fresh grass with grace. She really was gorgeous I found myself thinking, her thick locks messy around her face as she seemed to glow in the sun's rays which shone down upon us. Yep, she was a vision and I loved that I could call her my own.

Her question brought me back to reality though, my hands clenching at my sides as I thought about the conversation we were going to have when we got back. I hated that it would ruin the good mood we both seemed to have been in, I hated how she might jump to conclusions and I hated how I knew she wouldn't move in with me if her parents were there. Basically, this whole situation sucked.

"Your parents-" I started in a harsh tone but she cut me off, her tone both soft and firm as she did so.

"Don't call them that Hunter, please" she breathed causing me to nod, quickly reaching out to bring her back into my arms. I turned her so her back was firmly against my chest, my muscular arms wrapped gently around her waist as I pressed my face into her thick curls as I took a deep breath of her natural aroma to try and calm myself.

"Sorry baby, I apologise" I said honestly, not having meant to dampen her good mood with my comment. I was stupid enough to open my big mouth, of course she didn't want to be reminded of who those people were to her.

"It's fine Hunter, it's just I have never thought of them as anything other than two people who have hated my guts for as long as I can remember. They were never my parents, I hate them with everything I hold dear to me" she said softly as she seemed to daze off in thought, my grip on her tightening reassuringly as breathed in her scent. Her tone was so strong, so honest that I knew she meant every word. It wasn't a surprise to me for her to admit how much she loathed them, I knew Jack felt the same but Zoe just had more of a reason to hate them. Much more of a reason.

"I know, I'm sorry it just slipped out" I smiled, seeing the forgiveness in those amazing eyes of hers as she shot me a wink.

"Back to the subject at hand, spill" she demanded playfully with a twinkle in her eye, though I knew better than to think of lying or passing it off as nothing. It concerned her after all, I wouldn't keep anything from her if I didn't have to.

"They want to move in to see to Stacy's recovery" I stated, watching confusion cross her before a light bulb seemed to go off in her head as she started to pull away from me. I wouldn't loosen my grip though; I didn't want her running from me.

"Let go!" she snapped wildly, her feet kicking out as I continued to try and hold her in place. I could only hope she didn't try and shift with me so near to her, the last thing I wanted was to end up as a managed mess on the forest floor.

"Calm down Zoe, I'm not going to say yes to them!" I growled out when I felt her wiggling increase, only for her to go slack in my arms when she heard my comment. She clearly hadn't expected it and it pained me that she thought I would've let them stay.

"Really?" she asked hopefully, it was clear that while she didn't live there yet she liked to spend her time there when we hung out together. She loved the pack as if they were her family, it was enough for them all to see her as the alpha female she was destined to be as she stood by my side as we led it together.

"Of course Zoe, I don't want them there as much as you do" I stated, though confusion seemed to cross her features before her eyes widened in realisation. What she realised though I had no idea, until her next comment made my blood run cold and the colour to drain from my face instantly. Shit.

Chapter 31

- -

Zoe's Pov

"Why?" I asked flatly when I remembered that I had told him nothing of my past, that I had told him nothing of how those people had treated me and yet he was reacting like this. He shouldn't have been, he should have been at least asking me what was wrong, why I hated them so much and yet he talked as if he already knew. I paled at the thought, he didn't know, did he?

I stared at him as the colour seemed to drain from my features, his arms around me suddenly tightening as if he was worried I would run. I hated to admit it to myself but the thought had crossed my mind, I knew I didn't deserve him but the thought of leaving him was just too much to bare. I knew my wolf would be in immense pain if I ran, not to mention I felt way too much for him to just pick up and leave.

"I don't know what-" he started to stutter but I cut him off, not trying to get out of his grip on me but not relaxing into it either.

"Don't lie to me" I snapped, "so tell me, why do you hate them so much?" I asked in a clipped tone, my wolf snarling at me for talking to my mate in such a manner but I was far to panicked to think straight. How did he find out? Did he find out?

"Look Zoe-" he started again but I didn't let him get another word out, to worried that he knew more about me than I had told him. It wasn't like I enjoyed keeping things from him, but the realisation that he had found out elsewhere made my blood run cold as I stood stiffly in his arms. A first for me, and for him going for the expression on his face.

"What do you know?" I asked bluntly, quietly as I couldn't bring myself to look at him. I didn't want to see the hate, the disgust that would be in his gaze. I had done a lot of things I wasn't proud of, and not coming clean with him as soon as we started dating was one of them. To be honest though I was worried about how he would react, it wasn't every day that a mate had to listen to how his female was kicked out when she was a child and forcibly made a rogue at such a young and delicate age. I didn't know how he would have taken it, so I had kept quiet and now I was paying for it.

At my question he seemed to go silent, clearly not knowing what to say but as I looked into his eyes I saw genuine fear present in them. The sight brought me up short, what did he have to fear? I soon realised what it was though when I felt his arms tighten around my waist as if it was the only thing keeping me here. I couldn't help it as I looked into those bright eyes of his, knowing that he wasn't just fearing me pulling away from him, but he feared that I wouldn't be the one wanting him. Such a fool.

I sighed heartbroken at the thought that he generally believed that I was going somewhere, the thought had crossed my mind but he was stuck with me now. Now I had found my mate, my forever, I would never be letting him go.

With this on my mind I gently relaxed against him, letting my posture droop as my arms wrapped around his neck as I pressed my chest against his. I could tell the action surprised him, my sudden change of attitude having him stumped making me smile softly as I pressed my lips to the bare skin of his chest. I loved that he was hairless in that area, most werewolf males were which I found strange considering when we phased we were covered from head to toe in fur.

Hearing and feeling his chest vibrate with a purr I felt his large muscular arms as they wrapped themselves around me gently, as if he was worried that any sudden movements would cause me to run. I wanted to laugh at the thought of it, I may know he was too good for me but the last thing I planned to do was to leave my mate when I was in an anger filled state.

"Tell me" I said in a softer tone as I pressed my lips harder against his chest, letting my tongue caress his skin as I buried back a moan at the taste of him. I would never get enough of him I realised; I would always crave his presence, his company, his taste. No, he was mine and it was going to stay that way whether he liked it or not!

"You're going to hate me" I heard him mutter, my fingers playing with the back of his hair as I made a mental note to tell him to get a haircut.

"I can never hate you Hunter, you mean to much to me for me to ever hate you" I replied, trying to portray how sincere I was in my tone. It seemed to have worked, feeling his grip on me loosen slightly but he kept his arms around me, where they belonged.

"When I-" he started, his words catching in his throat. Never had I seen him so nervous, so weak and it was fair to say I hated it. He was an alpha, he was my protector and my mate, he wasn't meant to be fearful!

"I'm not going anywhere, Hunter" I breathed, knowing that it was what he wanted, no needed to hear. And it was true, he was never going to get rid of me that was for sure.

"When I first met you, what I did baby was just...I flipped out when realised what I had done, so when I found out that my pack mate knew you I lost control to my wolf" he managed to strain out, my soothing touches hopefully having a calming effect on him. I hadn't realised how much his bullying of me still played no his mind, didn't he know that I had forgiven him long ago for that. It wasn't like he had been enjoying it back then, it had hurt me deeply yes but he was her mate which didn't make it exactly hard for her to forgive him. He was mine as I was his.

"My brother" I stated as soon as I realised, fighting to keep my posture relaxed and not to tense up like I wanted to. Bullying me was one thing, but harming my brother was going to be a hell of a lot harder to forgive and forget.

"I didn't harm him baby, just alpha ordered him" he spoke quickly, obviously sensing my whirling thoughts. I couldn't deny the fact I was relieved, knowing that in that sort of situation when an Alpha feared the whereabouts of their mate then fighting for control was pointless. So no, I didn't blame him but I was more than a little relieved.

"I forgive you Hunter" I breathed, feeling his breathe on the top of my head as he pulled me closer, whispering how sorry he was. I tried to ignore the fact that we were both half naked, trying to tamper down on my suddenly lustful thoughts since my mate was howling for me to let his wolf claim her, to let Hunter claim me.

"He told me about you, about how you became a rogue" he confessed, strangely though I found I didn't mind as much as I thought about him knowing the details of my past. Didn't it bother him? Didn't he care that his mate had been a rogue for so many years?

"What do you know?" I asked gently, my fingers tugging at the hair on the nape of his neck causing a growl like purr to rumble from his chest. Yummy.

"About those people" he stated, spitting out the word 'people' as if it was the most vile word in the world. It didn't take a genius to know that he was referring to my horrible parents, the fact he had taken to heart that I didn't want to refer them people as my flesh and blood warmed me more than it should have.

I couldn't help but close my eyes as I thought back to when I was so young, when I was literally thrown out of the house. I remembered how scared I was, how I had repeatedly knocked on the door to be let back in onto to receive a beating which had me running for my life. How I had only survived due to being the daughter of an alpha, the extra power coming in handy when I had to fight for my life when I came across rogues who were vicious, who pounced with the intent to kill.

As the thoughts ran through my head I couldn't help but feel my eyes turn glossy, feeling my grip on my mate tighten desperately as I finally came to terms with the fact that I was no longer alone. I had a pack I cared for, I had friends, I had Hunter.

"Baby, what's wrong?" he asked worriedly, the concern dripping from his tone only making me more relieved that I had found some-one to grow old with, to share my life with. I may not have wanted a mate when I had to fend for myself, but now I had him I realised how lucky I was, how much I actually needed another to lean on.

With that thought I tilted my head up to press my lips against his, capturing his mouth with mine as I melted against him. He deserved so much better than me I thought, grabbing hold of his hair roughly as I increased the passion causing me to moan and him to growl viciously as I soon found myself pinned against a tree, my legs around his waist as he was making savage growls that had my toes curling and my heart beat increasing to an alarming rate.

"Uh" I moaned against him as I felt him grind the tent of his jeans against my core, feeling pleasure which I hadn't been aware was possible as he tore his delicious mouth from my own causing a whimper of disapproval to fill the air from me. That was until I felt his lips working my neck that was, his grip on the back of my thighs tightening as he pressed his chest against mine with a sense of urgency that had me reeling. I had really hit the jackpot I thought, my mate was a god.

"You taste so good" I heard him grunt against my neck as his movements never slowed; only increasing my arousal as I moaned along with him. I could tell he was just as wound up as I was, if not more so but I also knew we had to tone it down. I found I had nothing against him claiming me, but I would at least like our first time to be in a bed instead of up against a tree – we could try that another time.

"Hunter" I moaned out, trying to keep my tone strong but failing miserably. It was when I felt his large, strong hands hesitantly run up my sides I knew that I hadn't completely lost him to his wolf. His alpha wolf wouldn't have hesitated like he was doing, my heart warming even more so when I thought back to all the times where he had had to struggle not to mount me like I knew both he and his wolf wanted to. The thought made me grin, he was perfect and I was so ready to give myself to him. Just not up against a tree.

I tried again but failed as his name came out as a high pitched keen when I felt his hands brush the sides of my breasts almost innocently, even though I knew whatever was going through that head of his was far from being innocent. He was a bloke after all, not to mention a sexually frustrated alpha.

"God you feel so good my mate, mine!" I heard him growl out against my neck, my sensitive hearing suddenly picking up on another howl from the pack house. I could literally feel how much of an annoyance it was to Hunter as he froze against me at the sound, but I also knew they was the perfect opportunity to stop this so we could carry it on later. Well, that was what I had planned anyway.

"Come on honest, they need us to go back" I soothed, sighing out in both relief and disappointment as he pulled away from me. The feral expression on his face had me panting, his eyes black as the night and he was breathing as deeply as I was. God he looked beautiful, deadly even and I loved it.

"We'll finish this later?" he asked hopefully, his voice deep and husky making me shiver in delight. I nodded, watching a he seemed to shake his head to try and snap himself out of it before his eyes turned back to normal. I couldn't help but smile, so perfect, so incredibly perfect to me.

"Fine, come on" he grunted as he scooped my up into his arms causing me to squeal out in surprise, quickly wrapping my arms around his neck much to his enjoyment as he took off into the woods with me in his arms. Honestly, I had never felt happier.

Chapter 32

Zoe's Pov

I couldn't help but laugh as I bounced slightly in Hunters arms as he jogged us towards the pack house, a bright smile lighting up my features as I couldn't help but burry my face against his neck as I breathed in his scent. It was clear that he was still wound up after our previous make-out, his muscles tense as a low but constant grow rumbled in his chest making my wolf purr in comfort and delight at the pure sound of it alone. It was more than a little satisfying.

I didn't know what had him so wound up when we were in wolf form, my mind not yet being linked to his and such, but whatever it was I knew it had to be bad. When he had phased into human form the pure anger that had been on his face was impressive to say the least, hell I knew that if it wasn't for the fact I was his mate I would have ran away from him quicker than I could blink. He looked aggressive and violent, but oh so gorgeous.

"What's going to happen?" I mumbled against him as he slowed down his run to a gentle jog, his pace decreasing until he was walking with me still in his arms.

He seemed to stiffen slightly at my question, it clearly making him uncomfortable but I didn't let up nor did I take it back. If this mate thing was going to work then he can't hide things from me, even if I again felt like a total hypocrite due to me hiding about being a wolf and such. Never had I been more relieved that he didn't seem to mind, rather enjoying me being able to phase. That didn't mean that I was naïve enough to believe that the subject was over, he was going to approach it some time or another and when he did I knew I would have to be completely and utterly honest with him.

"I don't know" I heard him mutter causing me to frown. Moving my head slightly I sank my teeth into the flesh of his skin beneath his Adams apple, not enough to draw blood but enough for him to feel it as he jerked slightly against the sudden action. "Zoe!" he growled, his husky tone telling me he was far from angry with the action on my part.

"Spill!" I demanded as I pulled my mouth away from the flesh of his neck, letting my tongue trail over my bite mark to sooth any sting that might be present. I couldn't help but shiver when he growled again, the deep and dangerous sound sending pleasurable tingles through my body making me flush with excitement.

"Peter and Lisa wanting to stay for Stacy's benefit isn't the worst news I was given" Hunter stated making me tense, what could be worse than hearing that my parents wanted to stay at the place which was considered like my second home? I knew though that if Hunter caved, letting them stay then I wouldn't be going there anymore, I simply couldn't risk the temptation of killing them instantly every time my wolf could pick up on their scents. It wouldn't be long until they were a mess of bloody limp limbs on the floor, just how I wanted them.

"Then what is?" I asked, slightly worried about what his anger would be.

At this I felt his arms tighten around me harshly, not enough to cause me any discomfort but enough for me to grasp onto the fact that he was not only feeling protective but possessive over me, leading me to assume that it had something to do with my well-being. I was right of course.

"They want me to...punish you" he spat out through gritted teeth, saying the word 'punish' with so much disgust, so much anger that even I had to stifle a flinch from his tone.

Sighing I leaned my head back against him, not feeling it in me to work up the energy to be either angry or disgusted with them over what they had clearly demanded. To be honest it wasn't exactly surprising, they were trying to take the opportunity to hurt me but I knew for a fact it wouldn't work. It was foolish of them to even think it would get them what they wanted though, asking an Alpha to punish his mate was probably the most stupidest thing that a pack member could do. Not only that but it was suicide; you do not threaten the safety and wellbeing of your superiors mate, ever!

"Calm down" I soothed as I reached up to cup his cheek, letting my thumb stroke his cheek as I craned my head up slightly to look at him with a soft smile. He was so beautiful to me, so fucking perfect that it hurt.

"Why aren't you angry? Hurt?" he couldn't help but ask, his eyes glistening with confusion causing my smile to widen softly.

"I'm not hurt Hunter because it doesn't surprise me, I mean honestly, does it surprise you?" I asked with a raised brow before I gestured for him to stop, wanting to stretch my legs since they were starting to cramp. I hadn't realised how far out we were into the forest until now, but my legs were killing me and I needed to walk at least to stretch them out.

"I guess not, but that doesn't mean I like it" he grunted as he reluctantly seemed to put me down, keeping an arm around my waist as the material of his shirt seemed to bunch slightly showing more of my upper thigh. I could tell he had took notice since his deep growl rumbled through his chest as I stretched my legs out in front of me, probably not the best thing to do considering it only rose the shirt higher up on my form, unintentionally revealing more of my tanned skin for his eyes to roam over hungrily.

"I don't like it either Hunter, and my eyes are up here" I replied cheekily when I saw his gaze on my butt, his hands running up and down my sides before he walked behind me, stilling his large hot hands on my hips as we started to walk the small distance between the woods and the pack house.

"I like your arse" I heard him mutter before his hands seemed to creep down my body, the heat from his skin radiating through the bottom of the shirt as he cupped my half-moon cheeks causing me to gasp and jump away from him with a playful glare that had him smiling sheepishly.

"Keep on track Hunter" I snapped playfully as I clicked my fingers in his face, his hand snapping out as he wrapped his fingers around my wrist gently, pulling my flush against him as my breath hit his bare chest causing him to shiver.

"Why? I like what we're doing right now" he purred out as I felt his nose trailed up the side of my cheek before his lips brushed my temple, my breathing suddenly becoming a whole lot deeper and more ragged.

"Because..."I swallowed, trying to catch my breath as well as to try and tamper down on my steadily rising lust for my mate. "Because we need to get back, I mean the longer we are don't you think the more they will be thinking that you agree, that you should punish me?" I asked, not meaning to be cruel but knowing it would snap him out of it.

I was right of course, his vicious growl causing me to jump slightly as I suddenly found myself back in his arms as his previously steady pace had increased in to a fast jog that would have us there in minutes. It did of course, the pack house coming into view in no time as he kept me in his arms in a way which I knew he wouldn't be letting me go anytime soon. I only hoped that he had the sense not to move me in a way which would bunch up the shirt I was wearing, the last thing

I wanted was to flash anyone since I was going commando in a shirt that only reached my mid-thigh. Yep, I did not want to give anyone a view of the junction between my legs that was for sure.

Chapter 33

H unter's Pov

Walking into the pack house I gently let down Zoe before we greeted the pack in the living room, my senses having taken note of how they seemed to have decided to gather and wait for me there. It wasn't surprising, but as I reluctantly set my mate on her feet I made sure to smoothen down the shirt she was wearing as to cover her important assets. I didn't like to see her in so little clothes around my pack mates, in private hell yes, but in front of my pack it made my wolf snarl in disapproval. Her cute little body was for our eyes only, no one else's and I would rip them apart if they dared to look at her in a way that I considered remotely lustful.

Once I had smoothened down her clothes I grabbed her hand and gently tugged her behind me and into the living room, my fingers lacing with hers as I gently but firmly pulled her along. I wanted her with me; my wolf would just have to try and ignore the fact that the pack was about to see her wearing so little at the moment since more serious matters needed to be taken into account. Like the bastards wanting to hurt my mate!

Reaching the living room I felt my body tense as I took note of the presence of both Peter and Lisa, the bastards having the nerve to look at my mate smugly as she stood partly behind me where she belonged. She was everyone's superior but mine, and while she was my equal in every way it was only natural for the male of the mated couple to want to protect the female more so in a situation that threatened their safety. It wasn't anything to do with whether it was fair or not since it was simply instinct, the females always submitted to the male, even if it took longer for some than it did for others but they would end up submitting in the end.

My deep and vicious growl soon wiped the smug looks off their faces, the rest of the pack looking at me strangely since it was clear that Collin hadn't told them about why I disliked the pair so much. I was relieved, it wasn't his place to reveal anything concerning my mate if I didn't want him to. Since I was the alpha it was up to me how this was dealt with, and as my eyes scanned for my parents I had to prevent snarling at them when I saw the disappointed look they were sending my barely dressed mate as she leaned against my back, her slightly sweaty forehead pressing against my bare skin.

"What has been said?" I asked Collin as he moved to stand beside me with Ellie at his side, Ellie trying to see around him to look at Zoe only to find that my mate was blocked from her view. Zoe didn't seem to mind, my back muscles rippling as I felt her lips brush against the centre of my back making me shiver in delight and want. Fuck...

"Only that Zoe attacked Stacy" Jack stated with a wince as he stood next to Collin, trying to shoot his sister a thankful look for protecting his mate only to find she didn't even seem to be paying attention, her hands winding around my waist as her lips continued to map out my back. I couldn't help but shiver, suddenly hopeful that my mate would be staying the night.

"See even my son admits it, your so-called mate attacked my daughter without proper reason!" Lisa snarled, the mother of my so called mate rising to her feet as anger radiated from her pores.

"Do not raise your voice to your alpha! Now sit now!" I snarled at her, my tone full of threat and barely supressed anger as the whole room grew tense as every pack mate except my mate flinched the sound and feel of it.

"But-" she started to stutter but I cut the vile woman off, not even wanting to hear her voice right now let alone see her in my pack house where she definitely did not belong.

"No! Sit the hell down before I make you!" was my only reply as I cut them off with a snarl so aggressive that it had each male in the room pushing their mates behind them slightly in case of a threat. It was instinctual so I didn't comment, I would have done the exact same thing if I had thought there was any threat to Zoe.

Thankfully she was smart enough to do so, quickly taking a seat as she seemed to be shaking slightly due to being on the end of such an ordering tone. Bitch. I hadn't even used an alpha order and I had her shaking, it may have sounded cruel of me but I couldn't help but gain some sick sense of pleasure at seeing the woman who had hurt my mate in such a way suffer. I found it hard to care about the woman's well-being, to be honest I didn't see her as part of the pack anymore anyway and it was only a matter of time before they could fuck off and take their vile daughter with them.

Once everyone seemed to have settled down I took deep calming breaths as I tried to settle down my anger and frustration over the situation, trying to concentrate on the feel of my mate as she left soothing touches on my forearms and back as she effectively made me calm in seconds. I couldn't help but smile gently as I looked back at her, seeing her mirror my expression perfectly as she shot me an encouraging look that had me grinning.

"Now let's get back to business, who witnessed what happened before Stacy attacked?" I asked, knowing what had occurred but needing to know the different viewpoints. Truthfully, however much I was hating it I needed to know Ellie's side as well as Chloe's, Stacy was wrong to try and attack but if she was provoked then I would have no choice but to be more lenient on her, even if it was the last thing I wanted to do.

"She did not attack-" the annoying woman interrupted me again, but an icy look from me soon had her lips sealed tightly just like they should be.

"Now Ellie, what happened?" I asked as I stared at my betas mate, Collin growling slightly before he managed to settle down his wolf. I couldn't help but pinch the bridge of my nose, it was late and I wanted nothing more than to settle down for the night, hopefully with my mate in my arms.

"I don't know, once minute I was laughing with Chloe, Hannah and Kelly and the next thing I know Stacy said that she wanted to talk to Chloe alone. She just flipped out, I didn't- " Ellie stuttered out, eyes wide as Collin was quick to sooth her as he rubbed her back and pressed a kiss to the crown of her head. I noticed he shot me a look, clearly daring me to not believe her. I wanted to scoff, of course I did.

Looking back at both Peter and Lisa I raised a brow, taking note that neither of them seemed to be very smug at the minute before I drifted my gaze to a still shaking Chloe and an extremely pissed off Jack. I knew I wouldn't have gotten an answer from Chloe if I had asked, the girl was far too shaken up to think properly and I didn't want to put the poor girl under any more stress than was needed.

"Well, it seems as if Stacy is the one in the wrong. Doesn't it?" I asked the couple as I crossed my arms over my chest, raising a brow as my stand grew straighter as I felt my anger yet again consume me. How dare their daughter attack a pack member, a mated female no less! It was a punishable offence.

"We had nothing to do with this, we'll talk to Stacy and get this all straighten out" Peter started to say, trying to appear a lot more in control than he actually was. I hated the man, what kind of father puts their child, their daughter out on the streets and forces them to be a rouge? The man in front of me didn't deserve to kiss the ground my mate walked on, let alone sit in my pack house, our pack house as if he owned it.

"Why you little-" I started but shockingly it was my mate who interrupted me, her tone flat but hard enough to have a number of my pack mates flinched. I pushed back on the sudden pride and lust I felt for her, telling myself to think on it later since now was differently not the time.

"Now that's not exactly true is it, father?" my mate spat, saying the word 'father' with such hate, such disgust that I couldn't help but wrap my arms around her waist and pull her closer to me. I didn't like hearing such negative emotions on her lips, but I was far too interested in what she was implying to comment on it just yet.

At my mates question I watched as all the colour seemed to drain out of his face, a look towards his mate telling me the exact same thing. They were hiding something, and it seemed like my mate knew exactly what it was.

Chapter 34

Zoe's Pov

I could tell that as soon as the words spilled from my lips that I had everybody's attention, including that of the two adults sitting in front of me who I was ashamed and disgusted to call my parents. I hated them with a passion; they were revolting people who didn't deserve the right to even breathe the same air as everyone else did. Call me extreme, but it was how I felt.

Looking around the room I saw that I was indeed correct, I was in fact everyone's sole focus as they stared at me with confusion and shock. I doubted they even realised just how much the people they had considered pack, people that they had considered family were so sick in the head that they were constantly making mistakes that would make others pale with just the thought of it.

"Zoe?"

It was my gorgeous and very confused mate who spoke up first, his husky tone sending shivers down my spine as I looked up into those amazing eyes of his. I didn't know how this whole thing was going to turn out, but I had a feeling that it wasn't going to be good.

"Hunter" I replied flatly, reluctantly removing my hands from his body which seemed to draw a frown from him. I couldn't help but flush slightly, but chose to try and ignore it since there were more pressing matters at hand. Like the fact I was about to drop my parents in a whole load of shit that not even they would be able to dig themselves out of.

I could tell that he was aware that I was trying to stall, it wasn't because I didn't want to tell him what had happened but rather I was having trouble putting it into the correct words. I had to be careful with how I worded it; I didn't need my so-called parents picking holes in my confession like I knew they would try to if they could. They were sneaky little bastards after all.

"What do you mean, what are you hiding from me?" he asked with a frown. I hated seeing it on his prefect features, hating it even more that I was the reason it was there in the first place. But I knew that he wouldn't only frown deeper when I spoke up, unfortunately it would be my fault yet again.

"Do you want to take this, father?" I asked in a bitter tone, looking in the old man's direction as he swallowed audibly.

"Now Zoe-" he started but was cut off by my mate, my very protective mate that is.

"Don't, don't you dare try and talk yourself out of this. I will give you one chance to come clean, now" Hunter started in his alpha voice, it sending shivers of delight down my spine while it sent fear down everyone else's. Hey, you can't blame a girl for finding their mate hot, especially when you take a look at the handsome piece of arse in front of me looking all scrumptious without a shirt on. Can I get a yum?

"I don't know-" my father started but he was quickly cut off by a very pissed off alpha whose mood wasn't getting any better.

"Let me make one thing clear, you lie to me and you will be punished" Hunter snapped, his own parents then having to get involved instead of stepping by and letting him do what needs to be done. I stifled the urge to roll my eyes, though couldn't help the flash of jealously that hit me with surprise. I couldn't help it, how many times have I dreamed of having a family that loved me like that, how a family should? But do I get that, no; I don't because I have to have the selfish idiots in front of me who care about nothing but themselves.

"Son, I don't think-" Tom started, his father clearly not thinking this was the right way to go. I understood why of course, both him and Stella were close to my parents and I hated to think of how betrayed they would feel when they found out that their closest friends were such selfish and greedy people.

"Dad, don't get involved" Hunter said tensely, clearly having a lot of respect for his parents and not wanting to raise his voice to them. The jealousy hit me again in a flash; I hated feeling it but there was nothing I could do about it.

"I know you're the alpha son, but this isn't right" Tom continued. I could tell that my mate was losing his patience with them all so I quickly wrapped my arms around his waist, hearing him sigh out in comfort before relaxing against me. I smiled; I couldn't help it since I loved the fact that I could affect him as much as he could affect me.

"Dad, stay out of this" Hunter warned, but I could tell he was trying to keep a reign on the alpha tone. To be honest he was doing a good job at it, I could tell how much effort and control it was taking out of him to do so.

"Honey, perhaps your fathers right" oh god, now mummy's involved. I know I shouldn't want to sigh out in annoyance since she was a nice woman but I couldn't help it, it was late not to mention dark outside so I wanted nothing more than to either head home or hopefully stay the night. Though I knew that if my parents were staying here then it was out of the question, I would just have to head back to my crappy apartment where the fridge was utterly empty. I frowned, I really needed that job.

"Mother" Hunter said tensely, I could tell it was getting to him.

"Just listen honey, it is clear that Zoe has some unloving feelings for her parents and we have to do this fairly" she continued, my own brows raising as I couldn't help but be slightly offended that she was implying that I was lying. I hadn't even said anything yet and I was being labelled a liar, and as I looked around the room at the pack I now consider family I could tell that they seemed stunned as well.

"Are you calling my mate a liar?" Hunter spat, my eyes widening as my grip on him tightened.

"Oh course not, but..." she started but it was clear she didn't know how to finish, because that was exactly what she was insinuating.

"My mate does not lie!" was his firm reply as my mate snapped at her, my face pressing against his bare back as I tried to hide my smile from everyone. It was times like this you had to love my mate, he was such a protective wolf and I loved it.

"I'm not saying that-"

"Yes you are, and I don't like it!" he continued when she continued to dig her grave deeper, her sigh telling us all present that she had given up. It was obvious to everyone that I wasn't the only one who was relieved.

"Don't speak to your mother like that Hunter, you may be the alpha but you are our son" oh god...

The bantering continued for a few more minutes until I had heard enough, and by judging everyone else's expressions it was clear that they had had enough as well. They wanted to get back to bed, spend some quality time with their mates before getting a good night's rest before tomorrow. It may be the weekend but that didn't mean everyone wanted to stay up late, to be honest with myself I wanted a night in as well.

"Look we're getting off topic" Collin interrupted before I could, the beta being on the receiving end of a number of thankful looks including mine.

"I agree, now Peter I will give you the opportunity to come forward with whatever my mate clearly knows you are hiding before we hear it from her" Hunter stated, being his usual generous self. It was clear from my father's expression though that he wasn't going to cave as easier as we were all hoping. Me though, I knew that he wouldn't have opened his mouth since the consequences would most likely ruin both him and the dreadful woman he married.

"I don't know what you're talking about" was his confession, how honest of him I thought sarcastically.

With his answer Hunter turned around to face me, his eyes swarming with confusion and interest over what I knew. I also saw hurt though, hurt that I had hide it from him when to be honest it was simply because I didn't have the opportunity or time to bring it up.

"Zoe?" he asked softly, the amount of trust in his tone making me want to tear up.

"I can't believe you would stoop so low" I told my parents as I stared at them, watching as fear flickered through their gaze when they realised that I was about to spill the beans on their plan. I snorted; as if I would cover for people like them.

"Zoe" they warned but I was already on a roll and I was not stopping now.

"I told you that I wasn't going anywhere, but yet you wouldn't let it go you power hungry gits!" I snapped at them, seeing them flinch and loving it. Call me sadistic but I simply didn't have it in me to care.

"Zoe-" they tried again but I didn't stop, I wasn't going to. Who did stop me though was surprisingly my brother of all people, what he said next having a whole other effect on me.

"Will you just get on with it Zoe, nobody cares what your feelings are ok! My mate was attacked today and to be honest I wish it had been you!" he snapped, his anger getting the better of him and while I knew he didn't mean it the words hit me hard.

The entire room was silent as I simply stared at my brother, no one knowing what to say as I found myself frozen in place. His unwavering glare in my direction had my heart clenching in pain but I hid it well, feeling myself closing up and rapidly trying to re-build my inner walls as to try and block out the sudden emotional pain I was feeling over his words. I could tell Hunter saw me doing this, his anger filling the room to an almost suffocating level that had every shunning back away from him. Everyone but me, but I was too stunned to move.

"What?" was all I could get out, my tongue suddenly feeling too big for my mouth as my nails dug into the palms of my hands in an attempt to restraint from smashing something like I wanted to. I couldn't help it; I needed to get out all of this emotion I was feeling one way or another.

"I said-" he started but Hunter cut him off, his powerful form appearing in front of me in a flash, effectively blocking my view.

"I heard what said and how dare you! She saved your mate when none of us could, and this is the thanks you give your own sister!" Hunter snarled, it hitting home for Jack but the damage was already done. Never would I have ever thought that the last of my family would turn on me like he was doing now. I felt sick, used and broken all over again.

With that on my mind I knew I needed to get out of here, I needed space. But before I ran with my tail between my legs I snapped my head in my parents amused direction, not wanting them to be in the clear when they were a hundred miles away from being innocent. It was almost amusing to see the fear replace the humour when they saw my narrowed eyes, that's right, I may be wounded but that didn't mean I was going to be the only one crumbling down.

"Why don't you tell them, tell them all how you planned this happening, how you wanted to drive me away? I dare you!" I snarled before turning on my heel and running, leaving them all frozen into place as my comment seemed to stun them all. I didn't know why, I mean was it really that much of a surprise of what my parents were capable of?

My bare feet hit the softness of the grass before anyone knew what was happening, my toes digging into the slightly damp ground as I legged it into the forest. I wasn't crying, I didn't want to cry anymore but my hands clenched at my sides as I tried to control my anger. I would take anger over hurt any time of the day. Just the thought that my brother, the only person I considered my family would so willingly prefer me to be attacked cut me deeply. I knew that he was only protecting his mate, but to freely admit that the thought had crossed his mind made me want to do nothing more than disappear into the night and never come back here again. I wouldn't of course, if it wasn't for Hunter none of them would ever be seeing me again and that was the honest truth.

I felt my body shimmer and vibrate before my large white paws hit the ground with a gentle thud as I took off running, my legs burning with the sudden strain of it but I didn't let up. The pull in my chest was almost painful as I ran from my mate, it wasn't his doing but I needed to get away to think. All I knew was that it hurt, it hurt so much that my brother had verbally attacked me for no other reason than to make himself feel better about Chloe having been in danger. It was the sort of thing my parents would have done was the only thing on my mind as I disappeared into the trees, knowing that it wouldn't be long until Hunter would start tracking me down. I could only hope that he sorted out my parents first; karmas a really bitch when she wants to be.

Chapter 35

Zoe's Pov

I didn't get far until I felt myself tumble to the ground as my legs gave away under me, a pair of long canines digging into the back of my neck as a large wolf pinned me down with ease. I didn't like how unaware I had been with my surroundings, but the feel of my mate's wolf on top of mine more than made up for it. I was in both heaven and hell, and loving it.

I let my mind cloud over with lust, needing a distraction as I whimpered and purred from underneath him, knowing that he wouldn't be happy that I ran but knowing that he would hopefully understand my reason why. I needed to get away, my brother may not have meant it but it had hurt more than I liked to care to admit. He was the only person I considered to be my family, even if others shared the same blood as I did. As far as I was concerned they deserved to lose the lot of it, they could bleed to death for all I cared.

I was brought back to the present when I felt his large form move slightly, effectively mounting me as I could literally smell the pheromones he was giving off as I felt myself begin to pant as my wolf went crazy for it. We had waited far too long, I knew that now, but I couldn't help but buck my back legs slightly as I tried to get closer to him. He growled at me warningly after my more than suggestive action, his saliva coating my fur which only fuelled to spark my lust instead of diminishing it like I would have thought.

I wanted to hear him I thought with a frown, wanting to listen to his thoughts as he mounded me in a way that made my wolf howl in pleasure and anticipation since she knew what was going to happen next. I knew that there was no way in hell that he was going to leave me without mating with me right here and now. I didn't care that it was in the middle of the woods, that my clothes were shredded and that it was rushed and unromantic. I wanted him, it was as simple as that and I would not be letting him go until I got what I wanted.

I felt his canines dig deeper as he held me down, his teeth breaking through my fur but not my skin. I wouldn't have minded, honestly the thought made me shiver in pleasure and delight at him marking me so soon in the game. He was my mate after all, not to mention I wanted him just as much as he clearly wanted me.

I wanted to phase but I didn't dare with his teeth so close to me neck, my body shifting and squirming under his wolf as it only seemed to turn him on more. His thick coat brushing against mine as a constant growl-like-purr rumbled in his chest as he rubbed himself against me, coating me in his scent as he held me still as if I wanted to be anywhere else other than here.

Snarling I tried to buck him off, wanting to phase back into my human form only for his grip on me to tighten as he growled at me possessively. I resisted the urge to snort; there was no way in hell that he was ordering me about. If he thought that I would just be a submissive female to him then he had another thing coming, I would be his equal and nothing else, even if his possessiveness and dominant side turned me on beyond belief.

'Bloody idiot' I thought as I slumped under him, did he seriously think that I was struggling simply to try and get away. Was he that insecure?

Wanting to try a different approach I let my body go slack underneath him, slumping to the ground with a thud as I calmed down my snarling until it was a light whimpering in the back of my throat. Hunter could be a real pain in the arse sometimes I thought with a roll of my eyes, such a silly boy.

As soon as I had gone slack I instantly felt his grip cautiously loosen on my neck, his canines releasing their grip after a few minutes and I instantly took the opportunity to phase back before I was lying on my stomach in the nude underneath my very aroused mate.

I could feel his hot and sweaty breath on my bare skin causing me to shiver in delight at the strange but far from unpleasant sensation, the smell of his wolfy breathe though could be improved. I knew that he was taking in the sight of my backside most likely; if there was something I had learned it was that my mate had a pervy side much like any other teenage werewolf. The fact he was an alpha didn't help either.

Feeling the tell-tale sensation of the air moving around me slightly I knew instantly that he had phased as well, his bare chest soon pressing against my back as he pressed his body flush with mine. The moan that left my lips was something that I couldn't have prevented even I had tried, not that I was embarrassed or anything since the feel of his lips on my neck was more than a welcoming sensation that had me purring.

"Uh, Hunter" I moaned as I felt his sweet breath on my neck, no longer smelling of wolf but rather the scent that I had become accustomed to smelling on him. It was a mucky, masculine scent that made me want to groan at how it set both my wolf and my body on fire.

"I have waited so long for this, so fucking long!" he snarled out, his blunt teeth nipping at my neck as he ground himself against me.

My eyes widened of their own accord as I felt just how excited he was against my skin, the fact that we were both naked meaning that I felt every part of him. To be honest it scared me a little, but I knew that he would look after me so the fear I had previously felt quickly drained away from my body as I let myself become immersed in the feelings that he was bringing me. It was pleasure, pure and utter pleasure.

"I've waited for this the moment I found out you were my mate, wanting to be able to touch you like this, to feel you" he muttered almost to himself as he had me on my back before I could blink. I couldn't help but flush slightly when I saw his eyes hungrily roam my form, feeling the heat spread through my body as I resisted the urge to cover myself. He was going to have to be happy with what I had whether he liked it or not, what with considering the fact I was his mate for life after all. But I knew that I didn't need to worry with the thought of him not liking what he saw, considering the fact that his eyes were almost pitch black with lust as he stared at me, drinking in the sight of me. I shivered.

"You look so beautiful" he continued, making me smile despite myself as he leaned his body against mine, his elbows on either side of my head as his nose nearly brushed mine with how close he was.

"Hunter" I whimpered, my legs bending at the knee as he lay between them. I wanted him, no I needed him and I didn't know how much longer I would be able to wait until he claimed me like I knew both of us wanted.

"So beautiful" he mumbled, his nose pressing against mine as he nuzzled me in a gesture that was pure wolf. I whimpered. "Tell me you want this baby, tell me your ready for me to claim you as mine" he spoke huskily, the fact he was asking even though I knew it must be taking a lot out of him being my answer.

Before he could even think of moving away to give me any space which I didn't need I wrapped my arms around his neck, my fingers diving into his thick black locks as I pulled him against me so that our lips were barely touching.

"Make love to me, Hunter" I breathed, loving how he shivered. "Claim me, I want to be yours" I continued to speak, my tone now husky at the thought of him mating with me.

The next few hours were pure and utter heaven, he was so caring and sweet that I couldn't help but fall for him more and more as he made sweet, slow love to me. The passion was still there, but it no longer felt rushed as he finally sank his canines into my neck as he marked me for eternity in a way that made my toes curl and my heart to stop for a few seconds as I felt so much love for him that I couldn't help but express it with three words that I never thought I would utter in my entire life.

"I love you" I breathed before I could stop myself, tensing up as soon as the words had passed my lips which instantly had Hunter on alert as he rolled back on top of me. We had broken apart to take a breather only for my tense form and words to have him instantly on top of me, our sweaty forms instantly pressing together again in a way that brought back pleasurable memories that instantly had my wolf alert.

"What did you say?" Hunter asked, eyes wide with unrestrained hope as he stared at me. His expression caused my heart to clench and I swallowed thickly. "Zoe, what did you just say?" he repeated again, the hope in his gaze never wavering.

"I love you alright!" I snapped, not liking feeling so vulnerable. Apparently it was the right thing to say though since he stared at me with so such love and devotion that it made my eyes water.

"Really, you mean it?" he asked brightly, his eyes lighting up in a way that made him look even more attractive if that was possible.

"That's what I said isn't it?" I snapped, suddenly annoyed with my confession.

"You love me?" he grinned widely, my eyes narrowing in his direction slightly causing him to wink. "I love you too baby, I have for a while now" he admitted. This instantly had my attention.

"Wha-What?" I stuttered, feeling as if I was glowing all of a sudden.

"I said I love you too my mate, so fucking much" he grinned before crashing his lips to mine, a moan falling from my lips as he ravished me all over again.

It was about another hour later, both of us calming down yet again as we tried to get our breathing under control. I couldn't wipe the cheesy grin off my face even if I tried to, never had I felt as happy as I felt right now. I had a mate, a strong and protective mate who had just told me that he loved me. What else could a girl want? Sure a good family would be nice but I wasn't going to be picky, that ship had sailed a long time ago. I had given up on having my family on my side, I had my mate and that was more than enough for me to be ridiculously happy.

I didn't know how long we were sitting there until Hunter broke the peaceful silence, neither of us caring that we were as naked as the day we were born as we laid down by each other's side on the soft grass beneath us. It made me relieved that he had been smart enough to pounce on me at a clearing, if he hadn't of done then it would have been more than a little awkward trying to get down and dirty if you were constantly rolling onto thick roots or hitting trees. Yep, I have to say I am definitely relieved that he had pounced on me here.

"What was the whole incident about with your parents Zoe, you weren't exactly very clear with telling me what happened?" Hunter asked causing me to sigh, but to be honest I found it easier to talk too just him then in front of everyone else. Not because I was scared, but because I knew that hopefully he wouldn't judge me.

"I take it my parents didn't confess anything" I stated, opening one of my eyes just in time to see him shake his head.

"No, they were pretty much closed off" he stated causing me to roll my eyes, how surprising I thought sarcastically.

"Well that's hardly surprising. What do you want to know?" I asked, keeping my eyes closed as I soaked in the comfort that my mate brought me merely with his presence.

"Everything, I don't like you hiding things from me" he stated, I could picture him frowning but I didn't open my eyes to check.

"I didn't purposely do it, but it just never came up" was my reply, already knowing that I was going to come clean with everything right now to get it out in the open.

"Tell me" he replied softly, running his fingers over my bare stomach making me smile despite myself.

"I was walking to school when they pulled me aside, I have no idea how long they were waiting for me but it's pretty sad when you think about it. Anyway they threatened me, told me to leave you or else. They threatened Chloe, I dealt with it" I stated in a matter-of-fact tone, not prepared for the silence that followed.

"Why didn't you tell me?" he answered gruffly, his harsh but controlled tone making me snap my head in his direction as I blinked rapidly at his tense features and clenched jaw.

"Baby..."

"I mean it Zoe, why didn't you tell me? I'm not just your alpha but your mate, your boyfriend, your lover. Why didn't you tell me?" he asked with a raised brow, his jaw still tense even as I ran my fingers over it in what I hoped to be a soothing gesture.

"Technically, we weren't lovers until a few hours ago" I joked, trying to lighten the mood by failing miserably.

"Zoe!" he growled, a sigh falling from my lips as I threw my leg over his waist to straddle him, feeling his body react instantly to our new position and proximity.

"Fine" I sighed, "I was being honest with you though Hunter, I just never felt the need to bring it up until now. Never would I have thought my parents would have the guts to do it, then again if I didn't know what they were capable I wouldn't think they had the guts to toss a young child out on the streets either" I soothed, seeing him relax slightly much to my relief as his hands soon placed themselves on my hips as he looked up at me.

"I can't believe I actually thought they were good people" he stated in an annoyed tone, clearly frustrated that he hadn't been able to work them out until I had come along. I grinned, though it was quickly wiped off with my next comment.

"Your parents aren't going to believe it Hunter, they are elders of the pack after all and while I am your mate I am technically nothing but a rouge" I stated causing him to frown, I rolled my eyes.

"Don't talk yourself down baby, you're the alpha female now, my alpha female" he muttered almost to himself, his fingers rising up to brush against my mating mark sending a shiver of delight through me. I couldn't help but grin.

"All yours baby, and I wouldn't have it no other way" I winked, enjoying this no end.

"Good, because I'm going to be the only one to touch you" he growled out possessively, my eyes rolling as I shot him a cheesy grin and a wink.

"Calm down big boy" I soothed with a laugh, feeling his arms wrap around me before my chest was flush against his.

"I mean it Zoe, you are mine!" he growled, the sign of dominance from my mate making me squirm in pleasure. What was wrong with me? I knew if he was using that tone with anyone else then whoever was on the receiving end would most likely be shitting themselves, but me, no I was purring at the sound of my mate dominating my wolf like he was.

"I know, as you are mine Hunter. I have skills, if a bitch comes after you then they're going to find themselves ripped to shreds before you can blink" I stated matter-of-factly, wiggling my brows as I pushed on his chest to sit back upright. However much I wouldn't mind another round, that didn't mean it would do us any good if we got distracted yet again. We had the rest of our lives to make love, something that I planned on doing more often than not.

"God, I love it when you get possessive, makes me feel wanted" he growled out with a wide grin, my hand reaching out to smack his chest but he grabbed me gently but firmly around the wrist before my hand could reach its target. "Now, now" he scolded playfully, the previous serious mood now practically non-existent.

"Idiot" I stated, my other hand flashing out to smack his chest only for him to grab that one as well. "Hey!"

"Not my fault you tried to hit your alpha, naughty girl" he winked, using his grip on both my wrists to pull me yet again flush against him. I wiggled free before freezing, knowing how much me practically grinding against him was getting him more than a little excited. Bad Zoe, I knew that if we got started again then I wouldn't be able to stop and it was getting late.

"I'm your mate which means I'm allowed to" I spoke, poking my tongue out only for him to lick it with his. I scrunched my face up, wanting to kick him when he burst out laughing under me. Twat!

"Of course you are" he smirked before his expression turned serious, instantly putting me on alert. "About your brother Zoe-" he started but I cut him off before he could finish whatever he was about to say.

"I don't want to talk about it, I know he didn't mean it but...fuck it hurt Hunter, he's the only person I consider family" I frowned, feeling my lips form into a pout as he looked at me with soft eyes. Why did he have to look so cute, so understanding? Uh!

"It was only because-"

"Of Chloe I know Hunter, but you don't just blurt out something like that out of no-where" I cut him off again, frowning as I tried to move myself off him only for his hands to stay firmly on my hips, effectively keeping me in place much to my annoyance.

"He was angry and upset Zoe, his wolf was at the surface of his mind-" he started to speak but I found myself growling at him warningly much to his shock as his eyes widened briefly.

"Are you seriously saying that I deserved what he said?" I snapped, seeing panic cross his features before quickly speaking to explain.

"Of course I'm not, Zoe. It's just, I'm not condoning what he said but you have to understand that a mated male wolf acts differently to that of a female" he stated causing me to frown.

"Like what?" I couldn't help but ask, beyond curious as my anger was instantly forgotten about. At my question he sighed, leaving his head back onto the soft grass covered ground before speaking.

"Male wolves are possessive Zoe; even the thought of losing you is...it's just too painful to even think about. Trust me if something happened to you, I doubt anyone close by would survive" he stated so honestly that I couldn't help but feel my breath catch in my throat at his confession. "He can't help it, since I'm the alpha I have to control it, Jack like the rest of the males in the pack don't" he continued making me daze off into my own thoughts. I was only brought out of it when he pinched my thigh slightly causing me to jump back to the present.

"I don't hate him" I mumbled almost to myself, but he answered anyway.

"I know you don't baby, but it's getting dark you want to go home?" he asked hopefully, making it clear that he meant for me to come back with him. I sighed, while I had said I didn't want to stay where my parents were I was too exhausted to head to my small apartment so I just simply nodded much to his delight.

"There's just one problem though" I stated when something finally clicked, his brows raised as his fingers danced over my soft skin.

"What is it?" he asked confused, my teeth biting into my bottom lip as I stared at him right in the eye.

"We're both naked and neither of us has any clothes"

Chapter 36

- -

Zoe's Pov

I stared at my reflection in the mirror, taking note of the large bite mark that now graced my neck. I knew that only a werewolf would be able to see it, what with it not being deep enough for a human to take note of unless they stared at it up close. I was relieved; the last thing I wanted was the curious looks and questions from the humans about.

Shaking my head I found I couldn't tear my eyes away from it, the perfect indentation of Hunters teeth on the side of my neck where it met my shoulder. I didn't hate it; in fact whenever Hunter touched it I felt a bolt of pleasure run all the way through me.

With that on my mind I grabbed a pair of shorts and a loose top before slipping them over my pale red undergarments, thankful that for once me and Hunter were able to spend some quality time with each other.

It had been exactly two weeks when the news of how my parents had treated me had been made known to the rest of the pack. It had been two weeks since Hunter had marked me as his mate, so it had been exactly 14 days since I was made the alpha female of the large pack.

I sighed as I thought about it, glancing at my reflection in the mirror before walking into the bedroom which I shared with my mate. I couldn't help but shake my head as I saw him lying face first on the bed, his arm stretched across the mattress as if reaching for me which I thought was absolutely adorable. Not to mention he was butt naked; a definite plus.

Walking over towards him I didn't feel guilty in the slightest as I effectively shoved him off it, hearing his shout of surprize as he hit the floor with enough force that I cringed when I heard the floor board creak with the impact of his weight. I would have felt some sort of remorse if he hadn't of been a werewolf, hell he was an alpha which meant he was practically invincible when it came to my rough treatment of him. I knew he loved it though!

"What the hell, Zoe?" Hunter growled as he pulled himself up from the floor, letting his eyes roam over me before he frowned. "Where are you going?"

At this I sighed, clenching my jaw before grabbing a book and lobbing it in his direction. I didn't know whether to be relieved that he managed to dodge it, or pissed off that he had. He had quickly managed to get used to how I tended to throw things at him, I mean it wasn't like he even felt the impact even if they did manage to hit him before he could avoid the quickly moving object as it cut through the air on the way to its intended target.

"You're taking me out remember" I rolled my eyes, seeing his eyes widen before a light bulb seemed to go off in his head.

"Is that today?" he asked, wincing when I shot him a glare through narrowed eyes. "I take that as a yes."

"You promised, Hunter" I reminded him, because he had. When we had returned from the woods and actually found some clothes when my parents' true colours were made known, even if they tried to rapidly defend themselves. It had been almost pathetic to watch them try and explain themselves, Hunters anger getting the better of him and I was actually delighted with the sight of him beating the shit out of my father.

Unfortunately they were still in the pack, even if everyone was ignoring them when they found out that the child that my parents had said ran away, the couple who they had comforted though there 'rough' time had lied to them...let's just say people avoided them like the plague and for that I was more than a little pleased. Thankfully they were only there until Stacy made a full recovery; hopefully that would come sooner rather than later.

Stacy however was a whole other story, and while the closer pack members and their mates knew my reasoning behind it, hell the bitch had attacked the mate of a wolf for fucks sake, I knew that many were still weary of me.

But that was two weeks ago and that's where I wanted it to stay. As far as I was concerned it was in the past and I didn't want it to ruin what I had now. Even if my forgetful mate was quickly trying to come up with a way to make it up to me; I could practically see the cogs working in that handsome head of his.

"Well..." I sighed dramatically, actually messing with him now. Like I could stay mad at my mate when he was giving me the puppy eyes; something I both envied and loathed. He could get away with murder my mate could, looking all innocent and such...

"Let me grab a quick shower and we can go" he told me, a grin working its way on my features causing him to mirror my expression. Yea...we had a very strange relationship compared to most.

"Thank you, baby" I told him, pressing a kiss to his cheek when he made a move to walk past me.

"I think I deserve more than that" was all he got out before he crashed him lips against mine, his body shoving mine against the nearest wall as I moaned into his mouth at his taste. Fuck, this was something that I knew I would never get sick of.

"Urm..." I hummed as he pulled away, leaving me flushed as he shot me a wink. He was in the bathroom and turning the shower on before I had chance to shoot back a retort, his husky laughter causing me to growl as I stamped my way downstairs where I met Collin and Ellie in the kitchen.

"You alright?" he chuckled, clearly referring to my dramatic display.

"He forgot, can you believe that he actually forgot? Idiot." I ranted as I took a seat in the kitchen, slumping into a chair as I shot a wave towards an amused looking Ellie who was leaning against the counter.

"Forgot, what?"

"He forgot that he promised to take me out, today" I continued to scowl, it only deepening when Collin looked stunned for a few seconds before bursting out in heavy laughter that caused a grin to form on Ellie's features as she watched him. I knew just how she felt; it was hard not to smile when seeing how happy your other half was.

"He didn't forget, Zoe. If anything its being running through his head non-stop since he promised" he laughed, my shocked expression seemingly throwing him over the top as he was soon having to grip the counter as to prevent falling over.

"Seriously?" I asked dumbstruck.

"Yep"

"I need to apologise to him then" I muttered to myself, "I kinda threw a book at him."

"Ha!" Collin snorted. "I am so bloody glad he met you, he needs someone to put him in his place" he continued with a wink, Ellie giggling at his comment causing him to look at her with bright love filled eyes.

"He's right you know, Zoe. You're probably the only one that would get away with half the stuff you do" she giggled, my eyes rolling but I couldn't help but shoot her a bright grin.

"What can I say?" I purred. "He loves me." I winked, knowing how right I was with my comment. He was my mate; of course he loved me as I loved him.

It was a few minutes later when Hunter jogged down the stairs, a bright grin on his features as he was instantly at my side. Pulling me out of my chair and into a hug I couldn't help but throw my arms around his neck, pecking him a few times on the lips but pulling away teasingly when he made a move to deepen the kiss.

"Zoe!" he growled, but like always I chose to ignore him.

"What?" I asked innocently, as if I couldn't feel just how much lust he was sending in my direction.

"Stop teasing!" he continued to growl, moving forward for another kiss but I pulled away before his lips could press against my own.

"What's it worth?" I teased, hearing Collin snort as Ellie giggled. Hunter just looked shocked, though the amusement was clearly present in his eyes. Then again so was the slight annoyance; my alpha mate didn't like it when he didn't get his way I thought with a bright grin.

"Didn't I give you enough last night?" he growled against my ear, his tongue flickering out to taste my skin causing me to shiver. Still, I decided to play some more.

"Last night?" I asked with fake confusion. "I can't seem to remember, couldn't have been that good" I shrugged out with fake ignorance, hearing laughter from both Collin and Ellie but a furious growl from Hunter as I dashed out the kitchen.

All I heard him say, or should I say growl, before I was out the door was 'I'll give you something to remember' before he shot after me. I grinned, throwing my head back with laughter as I thought about how much I was looking forward to this date he had obviously spent a hell of a lot time planning. I couldn't wait.

Chapter 37

---

2 YEARS LATER

Zoe's Pov

"Hunter!" I screeched as I felt sweat pool down my face, my hair sticking uncomfortably to my skin as I tried to breathe my way through the pain. It was all my bloody mates fault! How dare he put me in this position! "Hunter!" I screeched out again.

Never before in my life had I expected my future to turn out like it had. It was perfect. After being tossed away from my family like I had been when I was only a little older than a toddler I had prepared myself for a life on my own, where I wouldn't be with a mate that loved me because I did not deserve it.

But now...now I knew how pathetic and truly horrific my parents really are.

Of course I had always loathed them, and whenever the taboo topic was brought up I refused to have them referred to as the people who had given birth to me. They didn't deserve to say that I was their child, their daughter.

While I had hated the thought before I was extremely happy with how my life had turned out. I was alpha female of a powerful pack, I had a mate who adored me and was a right romantic at heart, and now I had the final factor which was about to make our lives perfect.

If only if I could get it the fuck out of me!

I remember the exact moment that it had clicked that I might have a bun in the oven, that Hunter had gotten me up the duff. I had been sitting on the pouch swing next to Ellie when I had sprinted to the bathroom with the intentions to throw up, the fact it was only the start of the morning sickness being a joke Ellie had made at my expense before the both of us had frozen.

She had rushed me to the pharmacy and was buying me a pregnancy test before I knew what had hit me. I had drawn the line at her coming inside the cubical and watching me pee on the stick though.

We were close, but not that close.

Turned out Hunter had impregnated me. My first thought had been around the basis of 'what the hell' before it finally clicked that I could have the family that I hadn't thought was possible before. I couldn't have been happier that I was pregnant with my mates child, that I was truly putting my past completely behind me for the better.

I hadn't made a big deal of breaking the news to my mate; I knew he had been wanting to try for a baby in the first year that we had been together. Werewolves tended to get pregnant young, I mean why wouldn't we as a race when we only had one true mate to love and hold?

He had been coming back from a pack meeting, one which usually I attended but I of course had been swept up in the emotions and missed it along with Ellie. He had just gotten inside when I broke the news to him in the bluntest possible manner,

"Honey, you're a father."

To say he had been shocked would have been an understatement before he had fallen to his knees, his ear pressed against my stomach causing me to roll my eyes. It had been a tad early for that.

Smiling at the memory blocked the pain for a brief second before I screeched my mates name yet again in a high pitched whine. Where the hell was he?

"He's coming sis," Jack winced beside me as I squeezed his hand. "Ow."

I sneered at him. "I have to squeeze out a melon sized kid out my vagina, and your complaining about me holding your hand" I snapped at him.

Jack flushed but shut the hell up. Good.

"I still can't believe my sisters having a baby," he muttered almost to himself causing me to roll my eyes. What a sap.

"Do you want to check?" I raised a brow at him causing him to flush and rapidly shake his head.

He couched awkwardly. "Urm, no thanks."

"Good!"

I was brought out of my brothers' embarrassment when I heard the voice I had been waiting for, my head snapping to the hospital door as I saw an excited but nervous Hunter rushing into the room with an apology at his lips. I glared.

"Where the hell have you been?"

Hunter winced. "Sorry baby, but-"

"What was so important that you haven't been here while I'm trying to push your son out!" I snarled. Yes, I was pregnant with his son and the fact it was a boy only seemed to be a bonus for him. I rolled my eyes at his behaviour, who really cared if it had been a boy or a girl? But apparently the pack was looking forward to teaching him sports.

Hunter winced. "Sorry baby, but I'm here now."

Did he really think that the fact he was here now made any difference what-so-ever? Apparently my expression said it all.

"I love you."

I pouted at that. He knew I couldn't stay mad at him when he went all romantic on me. Bastard.

"You're lucky I love you-" was all I got out before I whined low in my throat when I felt another contraction coming on. Oh god...

The next few minutes were a blur of pain and tears. Who knew giving birth could be such a painful experience? Hunter may want a house full of kids but I knew he would not be getting that wish any time soon. One was an enough for now.

As soon as the sound of a baby crying hit my hearing I slumped back on the bed, soaked through with sweat. The pack was soon filtering in and my tiny baby was in my mates' arms as he brought him over to me.

"God I love you,"

It was a rare sight to see Hunter cry, but the happiness, love and devotion was coming off him in waves as he handed me over my son, it was enough to have my heart swelling even more for him.

"I love you to."

And with that I knew that everything was going to be fine, because I had everything I had ever wanted. A mate who I knew was going to propose any time soon, he couldn't keep anything from me, a new baby who I adored with all my heart and a pack who I enjoyed the company of. Hunter had banished my 'family' the moment he had heard the news of our little impending arrival.

I was an incredibly lucky girl.

CPSIA information can be obtained
at www.ICGtesting.com
Printed in the USA
LVHW021005211122
733502LV00008B/438